I0818195

I was riding right into the storm. There was nothing I could do about it now.

Nothing but keep going.

As I neared the house, I slowed Firefly to a walk. It would be inexcusably ill-mannered to gallop past someone's home, storm or no storm.

Walking Firefly around the side of the house toward the stable, I looked up toward the window at the staircase landing.

A young lady stood there, looking at me.

It was her.

It was the girl I'd seen last night.

Only this time, she saw me.

WRITTEN IN THE WIND

ALSO BY KATHRYN KALEIGH

THE BECQUERELS

Twist of Fate

When the Stars Align

Once in a Blue Moon

Once Upon a Christmas

A Wish Upon a Star

Written in the Wind

Scripted in the Stars

Destined in the Twilight

Promised in the Mist

Trapped in the Melody

When Lightning Strikes

Storm of Time

Midnight Storm

When the Moon Falls

Stormborn Angel

Time Tempest

The Heart Remembers

A Moment in Time

Moonlight Shadows

Rescued in Time

WRITTEN IN THE WIND

THE BECQUERELS

INTO THE MIST

KATHRYN KALEIGH

WRITTEN IN THE WIND

PREVIEW: SCRIPTED IN THE STARS

Written by Kathryn Kaleigh

Published by KST Publishing, Inc., 2022

Cover by Skyhouse24Media

www.kathrynkaleigh.com

To learn more about Kathryn Kaleigh, visit

www.kathrynkaleigh.com

Kathryn Kaleigh

1

SOPHIA BECQUEREL

I stepped over a two-by-four, my work boots sending up a plume of sawdust. The buzz of the table saws mixed with steady pop of air powered nail guns to create a cacophony found only at construction sites.

Stopping at a door frame, I dropped my clipboard to my waist and studied the distance of the opening to the wall.

"Here's your helmet, Miss Becquerel," Frederick said, handing me a white hardhat.

"I don't need—" Frederick put his hands on his hips. "Never mind." I took the hat, though I honestly saw no point in it. No one was working overhead.

"Thank you." I put the hat on my head and smiled at Frederick. He was a middle-aged man—gray hair, obviously handsome in his younger years and still accustomed to using that to his advantage.

It wasn't fair to him that I was coming in now after he'd already gotten this far. Frederick was a good architect, one of the best in the state and THE best in Natchez.

And just because I had a degree from one of the best

architecture schools in the country, didn't mean he didn't have more experience.

I'd seen the blueprints and I knew what he was trying to do.

I had no problem with him replicating a house built hundreds of years ago, but there were always things that could be done better. There was no reason not to take advantage of knowledge gleaned over those hundreds of years, especially since central air conditioning, running water, and electricity had to be taken into account. And not to forget a modern kitchen built inside the house, not in an outbuilding.

Besides, I couldn't help myself.

I put a hand on the door frame.

"I hate to ask this, but do you think you could move this door down about..." I held my tape measure to the floor. "four and a half feet?"

Frederick rubbed his chin and gave a valiant effort toward hiding his disappointment.

"Sure," he said, making a note on his own clipboard. "Not a problem."

"Thank you."

I stepped through what would be the doorway. This would be the study.

The tall French windows would look out over the Mississippi River. It was a good view. Better than Grandpa Jonathan's view.

"Quitting time," one of the men called.

"Who made you the boss?" Another man asked, but all the saws turned off and the sounds of construction turned to sounds of men tossing tools into their tool boxes.

"Nobody's gonna argue with the clock," a third man said and the men laughed.

"Looks like the men are quitting for the day," Frederick said. "I'll stay 'til you're ready to go."

"Not a chance." I turned and looked at him. "I can think better alone anyway."

"You sure?"

Frederick was probably trying to decide if letting me think was a good thing or not.

"Absolutely," I said. "When I'm finished, I'll walk over to Grandpa's house."

"Text me when you get there, will you? Your father would tear me to shreds if something happened to you."

"I will." I turned away, waiting for the men to leave so I could get focused again. I'd ridden out here with Frederick, so I could see his point.

It was a fifteen-minute walk back to Grandpa's. Five if I jogged it. I knew because I'd jogged it this morning before I drove into town to get a copy of the plat. Asking the clerk to send over an electronic copy had gotten me transferred to two different people before I'd politely been told that they didn't do that here.

As the men drove off, I removed the helmet and took a deep breath.

Now I could really get a sense of how the house was going to feel.

I was pretty sure there had been a garçonnière here at some point—many long years ago... certainly not in my lifetime.

It was in the perfect spot to catch the breeze coming off the river and it was just far enough away from what had been the main house—now my grandfather's house—to allow the older boys privacy. Living in their own apartment, but still on the property allowed boys to be on their own while still being part of the family and helping out with the crops.

I walked around a bit, checking the general layout. The house was just a skeleton at this point.

If I'd know about it soon enough, I would have been the lead architect myself. But that would have required me being closer than I was to my father and not just in physical proximity.

I hadn't planned on spending my first summer after college graduation in Mississippi. Top in my class at MIT, I'd had three job offers in the Boston area. I'd ultimately chosen the one that allowed me to start in September.

And all because of one phone call from my father.

He was retiring from the Air Force after a full twenty-year career and was building a house on his father's land.

The timing was a bit off though. Father's retirement wasn't until October, but he wanted the house to be move in ready when he got here. With his new wife.

My momma could not have cared less. She had married her college sweetheart when they'd accidentally reconnected on Facebook.

According to her, she'd searched for him after her divorce from my father, but hadn't been able to find him. Then through the magic of Facebook, he had gotten a spontaneous friend request. He had accepted, messaged her, and there had been no turning back for them. They lived in France now. I missed her, but I was proud of her for following her dream and not letting anything hold her back.

In that way she was my hero and my role model. I had no college sweetheart to reconnect with, but I had gone to Boston, an unfamiliar city, on my own.

Father and I had never been close. Always at work, the Air Force was his life. But to his credit, he'd always taken care of his four children, even after the divorce.

It was going to be dark soon. And despite my insistence that I could get to my grandfather's house safely, walking in the woods at night was not something I cared to do.

Still… I wanted to take some notes, so I sat on a bench, in what would be the parlor, the guys had thrown together for themselves and turned to a blank page.

At first the music was faint… barely noticeable. Then it slowly got louder, until I couldn't help but notice it.

It was classical music… piano.

It was too loud to be coming from Grandpa's house.

When I looked up, the bright setting sun was in my eyes.

My vision still blinded by the sun, I put a hand over my eyes and looked to my right.

I saw people… men… and ladies… Waltzing. The ladies were wearing long hoop-skirted dresses that swayed as they twirled.

A vase of fresh white roses was in a vase at my right hand, where a side table would be.

There were three couples dancing and one man standing off by himself, a glass in hand.

I closed my eyes, squeezing them tightly together. Oddly enough, it seemed to help the music fade slowly into the background.

But when I opened my eyes, the dancers were still there.

The room was fully furnished, much as I imagined it being completed. A fire burning gently in the fireplace. Tall windows framed with emerald green curtains. The furniture was pushed back against the walls.

The one man, dressed in what looked like a black tux with a white cravat, leaning with one elbow on the mantle, seemed to look right at me.

His handsome face wore a confident expression. I couldn't tell if he was looking at me or through me.

I pressed my fingers against my brow and closed my eyes again.

I was imagining things. I'd gotten swept away in visualizing the completed house.

Shaking my head, I slowly opened one eye, then the other.

The sun had dropped below the horizon now and again I was surrounded by the barely framed skeleton of the house.

I blew out a breath and stood up. My knees were weak, so I sat back down to give myself a minute.

It was going to be dark soon.

I needed to pull myself together and get to my grandfather's house.

I could talk to him about it.

He'd know how to make sense of it.

Grandpa Jonathan was the wisest man I'd ever known.

2

NATHAN LAURENT

The whiskey burned my throat all the way down while the music soothed my soul.

My cousin, Isabella, played the piano like an angel. Probably one of the best things about being here with my cousins was listening to her music.

Even now, my younger brother and two of my cousins danced with girls who were supposed to be at the main house with their parents.

The Becquerels had invited several families over for a spring picnic and, since they had traveled some distance to get here, they had stayed overnight.

My cousins were a bit rowdy for my taste… ironic since I was from south Louisiana—with its reputation for breeding men with a wilder nature.

My family had come up from New Orleans for the summer—or however long it took—to get away from the yellow fever outbreak.

Unless a person had had the fever and lived to tell the tale, they were not welcome in polite society. It was one of those unwritten laws of New Orleans high society.

Since we had not had the misfortune of coming down with the fever, we would have been isolated.

It made little sense to me, this being shunned for being healthy. But it was the code we lived by, at least at the moment.

"Come," my oldest cousin Martin said, "Join our dance."

"And who exactly am I to dance with?"

"I'll dance with you," my cousin's girl said over her shoulder as they twirled past.

I didn't hear my cousin's response, but I noticed that he led her away, not stopping long enough to change dance partners.

It was well and good enough for me. I was content to watch. Not interested in being part of their illicit affairs.

Unfortunately, I was relegated to bunking here in my cousins' garçonnière for the duration of our stay here outside of Natchez.

I suppose I could have stayed in New Orleans. I was a grown man after all. But I needed to speak with my uncle Samuel about some business in the Natchez area. Besides, my brother, the oldest son, stayed behind to take care of the country house. Grant was content to be left to himself. The more alone time he had, the happier he was.

So we'd packed up. My parents, my sister, and my younger brother and traveled with a caravan of wagons and buggies north. It had taken us three days to get here.

After only being here a few days, the Becquerel family threw this picnic to introduce us to the locals.

If you asked me, it did nothing but incite trouble—the possibility of it anyway.

My younger brother was going to be in trouble before the month was out. I would bet money on it.

Needing to get some fresh air, I stepped outside into the early evening air. The moonlight glinted off the Mississippi River. The same river that passed alongside my father's property near New Orleans.

The water moved quicker than it looked. The river looked, and smelled, more like a putrid pond.

Tomorrow I would go into town. Do some initial research.

I wasn't one to put things off and since we'd been here for a few days, I was itching to get moving in a productive direction.

That's when I saw her.

Not more than six yards away. The profile of a beautiful siren with long brunette hair flowing around her shoulders. She stood there, looking out over the river, much as I did.

As the seconds became a minute, the girl turned her head and looked in my direction.

But her eyes didn't focus on me. Instead, she looked right through me. As though I wasn't even there.

I blinked and she was gone.

A shiver ran through me, but I shook it off.

A trick of the light, trying to distract me from following through with my plan.

I shook my head.

Not tonight.

3

SOPHIA

I turned off the gas under the whistling tea kettle and poured steaming water in a mug filled with a hot tea bag.

Grandpa sat at the kitchen table, reading a newspaper article.

I sat down next to him, cupping the warm mug with both hands.

Grandpa set the newspaper down and looked at me from beneath his reading glasses.

"What's bothering you, Pumpkin?'" he asked.

"I was out at the construction site." I forced a smile.

"Is it coming along okay?"

"I think it's going to be good." I nodded and sipped the hot tea.

"But?"

On the way home and through dinner, I'd repeatedly told myself that I had imagined seeing dancers waltzing around the framed-up skeleton of a house.

Nonsense, I told myself.

"I think I might have had a hallucination."

Grandpa sat forward, looking concerned now.

"What kind of hallucination?"

"I don't know," I said, looking down into my mug.

"Sophia," he said and waited for me to look up. "Describe it to me."

"There were people... dancers."

"Where?"

"In what would be the parlor of the new house."

"That's odd," he said, sitting back in his chair.

"Odd that I had a hallucination or odd that it was in the new house?" I said with a bubble of humorless laughter.

Grandpa took off his glasses and pressed his fingers against his brow.

"The house," he said, softly.

I thought he was kidding. He had to be kidding.

"What else did you see?"

"There were three couples... the women were wearing long dresses... ball gowns..." I said after taking a deep breath. "and there was one man standing off by himself."

"Did you recognize him?" Grandpa asked.

"No." I shook my head. "They were all young. I think he was a little older." I swallowed and looked away. "He was handsome."

Grandpa nodded. When he didn't answer, I looked at him again.

"There's something you should know," Grandpa said, clasping his hands together. "Your grandmother—"

My cell phone rang.

"It's Mackenzie," I said.

"Go," Grandpa said, shooing me away. "We'll talk later. Go talk to your sister."

"Hello." Grandpa blew out a breath of relief as I walked away. He was humoring me. Trying not to make me feel like I'd lost my mind.

As my sister chatted, I walked through the foyer, past the tall grandfather clock made in the 1800s. A chill chased down my spine as I looked up into its blank face.

Grandpa said the clock was missing a part. A part that he had yet to find a replacement for.

I dashed upstairs to my room.

It was time to put this behind me and get back to reality.

4

NATHAN

It had been a long taxing day.

With black storm clouds gathering in the distance along with the deep rumble of thunder, I nudged my dapple-gray horse—Firefly—into a trot.

Firefly had been named by my little sister when she was knee-high to a tadpole and the name had stuck.

I could see the tops of the oak trees that lined the road leading to the house from here, so I wasn't far from the house.

The wind whipped at the new growth budding out on the trees. Spring came a tad bit later here in the northern part of Mississippi than it did down in New Orleans. Not that anyone would notice.

I'd been thinking all day about the young lady I'd seen last night. It had been for a moment, but I'd been drawn to her.

It was doubtless the mystery that intrigued me.

Being from New Orleans, I was not unaccustomed to the unexplained. However, I had only heard stories. I had never seen anything out of the ordinary myself.

Here I was thirty years old and I was only just now seeing something that couldn't be explained.

And on top of that, I was seeing it in Natchez, not even in the city known for its unexplained mysteries usually involving people from the great beyond.

I shivered at the thought.

Had I seen a ghost then?

She had been shrouded in moonlight, barely visible.

It was a trick of the moonlight. That was all.

And the fact that I couldn't stop thinking about her merely told me that I had been too long without a woman.

Even as I told myself that, I didn't believe it. There had been a dozen young ladies of marriageable—and dalliance—age yesterday at the picnic and dance that had followed. Not a one of them had tipped my interest.

I turned left and followed the road toward the main house. Hopefully I would make it there in time to avoid getting caught in the storm. Hopefully I could at least make the stable which was in the opposite direction from the garçonnière.

"We'll make it, big guy," I sat, patting Firefly on the neck.

The wind whipped at the gray moss hanging from the tall sturdy oak trees and lighting flashed in the distance.

I was riding right into the storm. There was nothing I could do about it now.

Nothing but keep going.

As I neared the house, I slowed Firefly to a walk. It would be inexcusably ill-mannered to gallop past someone's home, storm or no storm.

Walking Firefly around the side of the house toward the stable, I looked up toward the window at the staircase landing.

A young lady stood there, looking at me.

It was her.

It was the girl I'd seen last night.

Only this time, she saw me.

5

SOPHIA

The morning had dawned with a storm, cancelling any chance of construction for the day.

I didn't mind the time. I could use it to prepare for the Mississippi state licensing exam. Since my father was going to be living in this state, it couldn't hurt to get my license here, too.

After setting up a study area in Grandpa's office, I dashed back upstairs to get some papers I'd left in my room.

Coming back downstairs, I walked slower, my attention on the paper in my hand. A flash of lightning in the distance pulled my attention toward the landing window.

I stopped to watch as the dark clouds rolled in, bringing the rumble of thunder and the flash of lightning with them.

That's when I saw the horse and rider below.

It was the man I'd seen last night. The man standing away from the others who danced.

He pulled on the reins, bringing the horse to a stop.

Unlike last night when he'd looked right through me, he saw me now.

My breath hitched in my throat.

The man was dressed in black pants and a white button-down shirt, open at the collar and he wore a hat. Not a baseball cap, but what looked like what I would call a derby.

He was a handsome man, but I was used to handsome men. Working in the male-dominated profession of architecture alongside almost completely all male construction workers, I saw plenty of handsome men on a day-to-day basis.

None of them tripped off butterflies in my stomach like this man.

I'm not sure how long we stared at each other. Five seconds. Maybe fifteen.

He took off his hat and smiled at me.

I took a step back.

That's when the rain started. The man put his hat back on and nudged his horse forward.

I jumped at a bolt of lightning that crashed to the ground outside the window, a crash of thunder right behind it.

Getting away from the storm, I continued down the next flight of stairs.

As my right foot touched the floor, the grandfather clock began to chime the hour.

I froze right there. One foot on the floor. One on the bottom step.

How was it that in the span of mere seconds, my life had been turned upside down?

I'd seen the mystery man from last night again… the man who wasn't supposed to have been there to begin with.

And now the clock.

The clock that was supposed to be broken was steadily ticking, the pendulum swinging. The chime echoing through the quiet house.

I forced myself to keep moving, but I stopped to stand in front of the clock. It looked different. Cleaner. Then I realized what it was.

The rip across the front of the clock was gone.

The rip had always been there.

Being military brats, we hadn't visited Grandpa but a couple of times. I'd spent the summer once when I was nine and the whole family had come for Christmas one year when I was a teenager.

My grandmother had still been living both times. She was an incredible lady. Strong and caring. I regretted not getting to know her better. With my father working all the time and my mother trying to manage a household with four children, visiting her husband's parents wasn't exactly high on her list.

The house was different now with Grandma Vaughn gone. Like it was in mourning.

Grandpa was doing surprisingly well living on his own. Of course, it had been a few years ago now since Grandma's passing.

I turned down the hallway.

I'd ask Grandpa about the man and the clock. He'd know.

Lightning flashed, then Grandpa was standing right in front of me.

"You scared me," I said, putting a hand over my heart. "I didn't see you standing there."

Grandpa was looking at me as though he'd seen a ghost.

"Sophia," he said. "We need to talk."

6

NATHAN

The storm was one of the worst I'd seen. I couldn't help but wonder if a hurricane had come in from the gulf. I had no way of knowing, of course.

The oak trees stood strong, their moss blowing out like flags. But the pine trees weren't so strong. They flexed, but some didn't bend enough and they cracked.

I took care of Firefly, brushing him down after being out all day and gave him fresh hay. While I was at it, I tossed the other horses some hay, too.

The labor felt good and freed up my mind to try to process my day.

First, I replayed my meetings in my head. They'd gone as well as expected considering they were merely introductory in nature.

With that out of the way, I allowed myself to think about the girl.

I'd seen her twice now.

And this time I knew I hadn't imagined it.

She could be a guest, although that didn't fit with what I'd seen last night. A regular person didn't just disappear like that.

She could be a ghost, but I didn't want to believe that. I wanted her to be real.

I kept myself busy until the storm passed. There would be lots of trees and other debris to clean up. There would doubtless be damage to my uncle's crops.

Fortunately, it was early in the year and things could be replanted if necessary.

After the rain passed, I stepped out of the stable and surveyed the damage. It was almost too dark to see at all, but the full moon was already shining brightly.

A couple of trees were down on this side of the house, but nothing too bad. Everything smelled fresh after the rain. Even the leaves on the trees were greener.

As I walked toward the house, I looked toward the landing. The girl wouldn't be there. And if she was, it would be too dark to see her. Unless of course she was a ghost haunting the house. Did people usually see ghosts at night?

I held my breath, hoping not to see her, as I passed the window.

Then, as I went through the back door, I looked for her, hoping to see her.

I was obviously a little conflicted.

There was no one in the dining room, but I heard voices coming from the parlor.

Not wanting to get tied up with anyone, I stopped in the foyer next to the tall grandfather clock steadily ticked away the minutes, and looked into the parlor.

My father was there, talking with my uncle.

The ladies must have gone upstairs to bed early tonight. They were probably still recovering from the late night they'd had the night before.

If the girl was here, she must have retired for the night as well.

I tamped down my disappointment. It was for the best.

I was going to be busy over the next few weeks and wouldn't have time for courting.

And I certainly didn't have time to contend with being the only person here who saw a ghost roaming about the property.

Mon Dieu. It wasn't even something I could ask anyone else about.

If the place was haunted, I was more than sure that my rowdy cousins would have told me about it.

7

SOPHIA

I held the warm coffee mug in both my hands.

An unopened newspaper sat on the breakfast table, still in its plastic sleeve covered in droplets of water.

Grandpa had internet and a computer, but he still liked to read a printed newspaper. He wore a pair of jogging pants and a tee-shirt and in my opinion, looking quite hip for a grandfather.

Still, there was something troubling in his expression.

He wanted to talk to me.

I tapped my fingers, forcing myself to be patient.

"What's wrong?" I wasn't being very good at it. "Is someone sick or hurt?"

"No. No," he said. "Nothing like that." His expression changed. "Actually it's kind of the opposite."

I exhaled, letting go of some of the anxiety. If everyone was okay, then whatever it was, I could deal with it.

"What then?" I asked, attempting a smile.

"I'm not so sure where to start," he said, rubbing his chin.

"I guess you could start at the beginning."

"Okay," he said. "Let me start with your Grandmother Vaughn."

"Oh." I sat back. This was going to be painful, after all.

"I don't think she's really gone."

"Grandpa." I reached out and put a hand over his. "I'm so sorry."

"No," he said. "She's gone back in time."

I pulled my hand back and looked at him. Maybe I should call someone. My father. Grandpa was getting up in age, but he'd never shown any signs of cognitive decline.

"What do you mean?" I needed to know more before I jumped to conclusions.

"She was born in the 1700s. In France. She came to America as a young girl to get married. But once she got here, her traveling party was set upon by hostile Indians and everyone else was killed."

"She was the only one who survived? How?"

"An old Indian, not one of the hostiles, cast a spell. The spell made a rip in time and she went through it."

I didn't want to interrupt him, so I just listened.

"She went to the 1800s for a time, then came here."

"Grandpa?"

"The spell is very strong within her. She has no control over it. No control over when or where she travels. But it's usually here or back in the 1800s."

"Are you saying she could come back? Here?"

"It's possible. And I'll go to my grave waiting for her. But that's not why I'm telling you this."

I had a really bad feeling about what he was about to tell me. A very bad feeling.

"You have Vaughn's blood, so you carry the spell."

I sat back in my chair and stared blankly into my coffee mug at the coffee that was getting cold by the minute.

"What does that mean?"
"It means you could go back in time."
"Could?" I looked blankly at him.
"Maybe you already have."

8

NATHAN

I stayed busy over the next few days, much of it spent riding my uncle's property, first without him, then with him.

The man had amassed so many acres, it was unreal.

We came to an agreement fairly easily. Uncle Samuel was a peaceful, reasonable man who knew that he had more property than he or his children could ever use. So he was generous in bestowing some of what he had to his one nephew who showed an interest in the land.

My older brother would never come north. He was completely wrapped up in the New Orleans property. There was no accounting for what my younger brother would do. Right now he was sowing his wild oats.

And my sister would marry a man who would take care of her. Not now. Right now she was too young. But one day when the time was right.

I sat in my uncle's study, head bent over his desk, pen in hand.

My fingers were stained with ink.

I was good with numbers and plans, but I preferred being outside doing the physical work.

What I was proposing took both.

A grand scheme. Unlike anything else around here.

I could do it down south on my father's land in New Orleans, but I didn't want to. I wanted to do it my way—without my father's input. And he would offer it. And whether he intended it to or not, his input would alter may plans.

My uncle, on the other hand, would let me do things my way. Part of it was because I was his nephew and not his son. The other part of it was his personality. He was more easygoing. Could be why his sons were so rowdy.

At any rate, I had come to the conclusion that the only way the south was going to prosper was to make its own factories.

Why we shipped all our cotton north to the factors, then bought their cloth was beyond me. We had the capability to build and run our own textile mills. Yet we didn't do it. So I'd taken it upon myself to study. To figure out a plan.

I had the funds. That wasn't a problem. I needed to procure the materials, hire the men to build it, and hire workers to run it.

I'd buy cotton from my uncle and even my father. It was a win-win. I could sell cloth to the local merchants at a lower price because I didn't have to ship everything north and then back again.

I turned the large piece of paper, sketched in some details.

My thoughts wandered back to the girl. I hadn't seen her these past few days.

But I'd watched for her. And I'd listened. I'd listened for anyone to say anything that even hinted that someone else had seen her.

But I'd heard nothing. No one else mentioned anything about seeing a ghost or a girl.

So I hunkered down and moved forward with my plan.

I think I perplexed my family because I was a doer and not a talker. They said I took after my grandfather. My grandfather on my mother's side was the one who had decided to plant crops. He'd thought it and he did it and now his family was reaping the rewards that he'd only had a handful of years to enjoy.

When I decided to do something, I did my research, laid out my plans, and moved forward.

Unlike my grandfather, I wanted to be successful at a young age. And unlike my father, I wasn't willing to coast on the coattails of those who came before.

I knew I was fortunate they had given me what they had.

Irritated at my own thoughts, I got up and stretched. It was time for a break.

Maybe it was time for me to think about finding a wife and settling down. Maybe that would calm some of the unrest I was feeling as of late.

9

SOPHIA

It was a beautiful morning. And by all rights, I should be out at the construction site.

Even from the breakfast room of my grandfather's house, I could hear the saw running and the steady pounding of the nail guns. Every now and then I could even hear men's voices.

But after due consideration of what my grandfather had told me, I'd decided that it wasn't safe for me to stay here.

I still wasn't sure whether or not I believed all the talk of time travel, but I had to ere on the side of caution.

If—a big if—my grandmother had gone back in time and if the spell—perhaps more like a curse—had saved her life by sending her through time… and if—the scary one—I carried the spell in my blood or however it worked, then I could not risk staying here.

I had a career. And plans. I was a licensed architect with a new job starting in the fall.

Going back in time was not in my plans.

I gazed out the window overlooking the back yard as I sipped my hot coffee.

My luggage was packed and in the car. My purse and phone were in the car.

I was ready to go.

Just waiting for Grandpa to come downstairs to see me off.

He'd taken a phone call, said it was important, and he would be right down.

I could wait. I was early.

My heart was heavy. I'd planned on spending the summer here. Spending time with my grandfather… working on the design of my father's house… even getting my license here in Mississippi.

Then I would be ready to start my job in the fall.

I had plans.

Finished with my coffee, I rinsed my cup and put it in the dishwasher.

I walked toward the front of the house. As I passed the staircase, I could hear my grandfather's muffled voice. I avoided looking at the grandfather clock as I kept going into the parlor.

As I walked, I soaked in the design of the house. The tall archways. The tall French windows. I loved the style and found myself incorporating it into projects.

I toyed with the remote control, bringing up the Weather Channel. After a commercial advertising a new action movie, the local forecast flashed across the screen.

There was a storm coming in.

Where had that come from?

I would be driving right into it.

When I'd checked last night, the radar had been clear. No chance of rain today.

The construction workers hadn't known it either or they wouldn't have come out. This meant they would be packing it in soon.

I stood at the window and watched as the dark clouds moved overhead.

Well hell. It was not only going to rain… it was going to storm.

If I was going to leave, I needed to do it. I looked at the radar again. If I left now, I could still get ahead of the storm.

Putting the remote down, I went to the bottom of the stairs and looked up. Grandpa was still talking.

I dashed up the stairs and went to the open door of his bedroom study. He was pacing, the phone to his ear.

When he turned, he saw me standing there and held up a finger.

I nodded and shrugged. Wandered to the window at the end of the hallway and looked out. The wind whipped at the silver moss hanging from the trees and sent fallen leaves and dust swirling about.

A couple of the smaller pine trees bent over as a gust of wind swept through and rain drops splattered against the glass. Original glass panes, I noted, from the original house. I could tell because they were thick and wavy.

It wasn't a good time for me to be leaving right now anyway. I'd missed my window.

I needed to go out to the car and get my purse… my phone. Maybe I should go now before the storm got any worse.

I headed downstairs and slowed at the foot of the stairs.

There was a loud pop and then the electricity went out.

I froze.

The house was dark, lit only by what was left of the dim light of day that survived the storm.

I jumped as the grandfather clock began to chime.

The broken clock…

Chimed the hour…

10

NATHAN

I left my uncle's study and wandered to the back door and looked out the window. It was a beautiful day, the bright sunlight glittering across the back lawn. The day was much too pretty to be cooped up inside.

But it was nearly time for dinner, so the sun would be on its way down shortly.

I'd put my papers away and poured myself a whiskey. Sat out on the back veranda and enjoyed a good cigar.

I headed back to the study and stopped in the doorway.

She was standing there, on the other side of the desk, in profile just like the first time I'd seen her.

Seeing me, she turned and looked right at me. Blinked. She had the most beautiful clear green eyes the color of a spring field I had ever laid eyes on.

"Good evening," I said, my voice sounded a whole lot calmer than I felt.

"Hi." She blinked again and swallowed hard.

"I've seen you before."

She nodded. "I know."

"Would you like to sit?" I asked, nodding toward the nearest chair.

She dropped into it and stared out the window.

"There was a storm," she said.

I sat next to her.

She was a beautiful young lady, but there was something different about her. Different from other girls. Her skin looked smooth as silk and her hair was long and straight. Not pulled back in the current style.

It was quite becoming.

She was dressed differently, too.

She was wearing denim pants that hugged her curves and a plain white tee-shirt with the painting of a teddy bear right there on the front of it.

The painting was extraordinarily detailed, but someone, the artist perhaps, had dripped blue paint across the shoulder.

"That's a nice painting," I said, pulling my eyes back to her eyes.

"What?" She crossed her arms across her chest, covering up the painting of the teddy bear.

"The painting on your shirt."

"Oh," she said with a little smile. "Thank you."

"My name is Nathan Laurent."

"I'm Sophia Becquerel."

I sat back, startled. "How are you related to my cousins?"

"I don't know. Who are your cousins?"

"Martin and George."

"I don't know them."

"Seriously?" How could she not know them when she was in their house?

"No," she said.

"Who's your father?"

"General Daniel Becquerel."

"General?"

She nodded.

"Texas?"

"What? No."

"I see," I said. Though I didn't see. What I did see was a beautiful young lady who looked completely lost.

11

SOPHIA

Things were not as they should be.

The grandfather clock—the broken clock—steadily ticked the minutes away.

And now the man I'd seen standing in a house that didn't yet exist sat next to me, making what sounded like polite conversation.

At first I'd thought the electricity had gone out. Then I had realized that there were no electric light fixtures to go out. There was no television.

Grandpa had prepared me for this.

As much as I had tried to avoid it and as much as I wasn't sure it was really a thing, I knew. I knew it had happened to me.

I had gone back in time.

My conversation with Nathan was about to get me in trouble.

If I didn't come up with an explanation for why I was here, then whoever lived here now might decide I was an intruder.

Being turned out in whatever year I was in would be

nothing less than a disaster. Grandpa had said the location of the house itself had something to do with the time travel.

"Actually," I said, pressing my fingers against my forehead. "I don't even know how I got here."

"You're lost," he said.

"Yes," I said with relief. "I have no idea where I am."

It wasn't even a lie. I didn't know where I was. It was possible I'd gone back in time, but I really didn't know.

Nathan seemed to consider.

"What is the last thing you remember?"

I decided to go with honesty as much as I could.

"A really bad storm."

He nodded.

"That's when I saw you," he said. "In the window. On the landing."

"Yes. I remember that."

"And nothing after that?"

"Nothing."

"It will be okay," he said. "We'll find out who you are."

"I don't know," I said, looking up at him from beneath my lashes. I wasn't sure if him finding out who I was would be a good thing or not.

"If not, I'll take you in. I'll keep you safe."

"That's very kind of you. But I couldn't impose on you like that."

I hoped I didn't need to. I hoped I could simply get back to my time, get to my car, and go. Just like I had planned.

"It's not an imposition," he said. "You're obviously somehow related to my cousins. They will certainly recognize you. I'll go now and see if I can find one of them. Someone who might know you."

"No," I said quickly, putting a hand on his.

An electrical current shot through me at his touch and I froze.

He glanced down at our hands, then locked his gaze back on mine.

"Did you...?" I asked, pulling my hand back.

"Yes."

"It must be the electricity in the air. From the storm."

He was looking at me sideways.

"The storm," he said.

"Yes." But the evening sun was streaming through the window. No evidence of the storm remained.

"It was raining," I insisted.

Shaking his head, he smiled slowly.

"It was a beautiful day," he said. "No storm."

12

NATHAN

The girl—Sophia—was not only lost, she was terribly confused.

"How is it you remember your name?" I asked.

Her beautiful green eyes widened.

"I don't know," she said.

"Are you sure about it?"

She pulled her gaze away and stared out the window.

I was still amazed at how much more beautiful she was up close than she had been the couple of times I'd seen her from a distance. When I'd thought she was a ghost.

But when she'd touched me, any remaining doubt that she was real dissipated. It had felt like an electrical current shooting through me when her hand touched mine.

"Yes," she said, then looked at me again. "But I don't think I'm supposed to be here."

"What do you mean? Why not?"

She shook her head. "It's just one of those things I know. I can't explain it."

I sat back.

"So if you don't think you're supposed to be here and you

don't want me to ask my cousins about you…." I leaned forward again. "What am I to do with you?"

"I just need… to… I need a little time to figure things out."

"I'm certain the Becquerels could help you."

"No," she said again, but didn't touch me.

"Well, I can't hide you from them."

She stood up, walked to the window, then turned back to me.

"How is it you're here if you aren't a Becquerel?" she asked.

"My family is visiting my cousins for the summer."

"Then tell them I'm your friend."

"My friend? If they recognize you, that won't work."

"No," she said. "They won't recognize me."

I stood up. Walked around to the liquor cabinet and took out a bottle of whiskey and a glass.

I poured whiskey into the glass and swallowed it, enjoying the burn all the way down.

"You going to share?" she asked, taking a step forward.

"There's only whiskey in here," I said.

"Okay."

"You want a whiskey?"

"That would be nice. Thank you."

I took out another glass and filled it. Handed it to her.

She swallowed it down. Impressive. I'd seen women drink whiskey before, but never a lady.

"Thank you." She set the glass down and walked back to the window.

I poured myself another one.

"The trees look different," she said. "Smaller."

I chose to ignore that comment.

"Do you know where you're from?" I asked.

"Boston," she said after a moment's hesitation.

Perhaps she was having trouble remembering that, too.

"How do you know?"

She turned back to face me.

"Some things I can remember, but not everything."

"Were you in some kind of accident? Maybe while traveling here?"

"I don't think so, but maybe."

"Who did you travel with?"

"No one." She bit her lip. "Actually I think maybe… I traveled with my grandfather."

"So you traveled here from Boston with your grandfather?"

"Yes. I think so."

"Where is he?"

"I don't know."

I sat back down.

"So… again. I have to ask. What am I supposed to do with you?"

13

SOPHIA

Nathan was right. There was no sign of any recent rain. Yet, I had seen it. And not just a rain, but a storm.

The trees were smaller, but there were more of them.

They'd been thinned out over the years, perhaps.

"I just need some time to figure out what I'm supposed to do."

"Alright," he said. "How much time do you need?"

"I'm not sure."

"And you're sure my cousins or my uncle or my aunt won't recognize you?"

"I'd be surprised if they did."

"Do you know what you're doing here?"

She shook her head.

"Well, I can't just hide you in here."

"I need to get back," I said.

There was someone coming down the hall. I stood very still, as though that would keep the person coming this way from seeing me.

A lady, dressed a long full dress stopped in the doorway. Looked at Nathan. Then at me.

"Hello," she said. "I didn't realize we had a caller."

"Oh, I'm not—"

"Aunt Eloise," he said. "this is my… friend, Sophia."

"Hello Sophia," Aunt Eloise said.

"It's a pleasure to meet you Mrs. Becquerel."

"Has my nephew offered you any refreshments?"

"No, but I'm good."

"Nathan," she said. "At least get the girl something to eat. She looks famished. We'll be in the parlor."

I bit my lip.

"Come with me, Sophia."

I did as she asked. The woman obviously wasn't going to take no for an answer, anyway.

I followed her down the hall. Past the ticking grandfather clock in the foyer.

Into the foyer with no television.

"Please, have a seat," she said.

I sat in an armchair in front of the fireplace and Mrs. Becquerel sat across from me.

"Tell me how you met my nephew," she said.

"It was quite by accident," I said, pleased with my quick thinking.

Nathan came in with a small tray of fruit and cheese in one hand and a glass pitcher in the other. He set both on the coffee table. Looked from one of us to the other.

"Surely you can tell me where you met," Aunt Eloise said, her gaze pinning mine. It was clear she demanded an answer.

"It was at the construction site," I blurted. And now I wasn't so pleased with myself.

Nathan moved to stand next to me.

"I'm afraid she doesn't know about the construction yet," he said.

Aunt Eloise shifted her pointed gaze to Nathan.

"Nonsense. Your uncle tells me everything. It's what makes for a good marriage."

"I'll keep that in mind," Nathan said, then looked down at me. "You hear that, dear?" he asked me.

"What?" I looked up at him.

He bent close to me.

"It's ok," whispered. "I think we can tell Aunt Eloise."

I shook my head, but it was too late.

Nathan took my hand and knelt next to me. Looked at his aunt and spoke softly.

"Sophia and I are to be married."

14

NATHAN

I doubted I would never know what had come over me.

But with my aunt Eloise peering at Sophia in a way that felt like a punch to the stomach, I went into protective mode.

I had only just met Sophia, but I couldn't bear the thought of her having to endure questions from my family.

They would probably send for the doctor. Start making inquiries with the neighbors. In short, they would put her through hell.

I couldn't have it.

So I went with the first thought that occurred to me.

I claimed to be betrothed to her.

"Please forgive us," I said. "but Sophia is exhausted and I was about to show her to the guest room. You will forgive us, won't you Aunt Eloise?"

"Of course," Aunt Eloise said. I had caught my aunt in a moment of sheer surprise, otherwise she would have insisted that I give her more details.

But I had to give her credit. After a moment of obvious shock, she kept her face impassive.

"I'll bring the refreshments to your room," I said to Sophia. "and leave you to get some rest." I looked back to Aunt Eloise. "Please forgive us."

I gathered up the tray and the glass pitcher and held out an arm to Sophia.

"Ready, my dear?" I asked. I normally would have been concerned about just how easily the words rolled off my tongue, but there wasn't time for me to think.

She stood up and hesitantly put her hand in the crook of my arm.

We left my aunt and headed back through the foyer to the stairs.

The grandfather clock began to chime the hour. Three o'clock.

My timing was accidentally impeccable. Three o'clock was the perfect time for an afternoon nap.

She watched me from the corner of her eyes as we went upstairs and I led her to what I knew was an empty guest room.

The door stood ajar so I pushed it open with my elbow and waited for her to enter first.

Her manner of dress was most unusual. I would have said she was dressed in boy's clothing, but even a boy didn't wear pants that hugged the body as closely as she wore.

It was quite flattered and sent my imagination down a most ungentlemanly direction.

I set the tray and pitcher on the little table in one corner and, facing her, braced myself for what would no doubt be a scathing reaction to telling my aunt that we were betrothed.

She looked at me with those lovely green eyes that tipped me off balance.

"Thank you," she said.

"My apologies." The words were so poised on the tip of my tongue that I hadn't had the wherewithal to adjust them before I spoke.

"No need to apologize," she said. "It was very kind of you. Your aunt was most intimidating."

I laughed softly.

"Fortunately, I caught my aunt completely off guard, otherwise, we would have been forced to come with a story right there on the spot."

I took two glasses from the tray and filled them with water.

"Sit with me," I said, holding out a chair for her.

She hesitated, but sat in the chair and took one of the glasses of water.

Using the little tongs, I made her a cheese plate and set it front of her, then made one for myself.

"I would behoove us to come up with a plausible story about how we came to be engaged."

"This should be interesting," she said, taking a piece of cheese and biting into it.

"Yes," I said. "It should."

This girl was nothing like I expected. Nothing at all.

15

SOPHIA

I sat with Nathan at the little table and nibbled on squares of cheese. The cheese was like none I had ever had before. It was tangy and sweet all at once.

The room was the very same room I used in my own time. It was the same, yet different.

The window was open, letting in a soft breeze that fluttered the light blue curtains. The bed was much the same. In fact, it could have easily been the very same bed, though the quilt draped over the foot was definitely different.

Also, there were no light fixtures and the door leading to the bathroom wasn't there.

That was one of the first things I noticed simply because I'd been looking.

Not only was I trained to look at how the room was designed, I looked because I needed to know if I was in a different time. If I was in the past.

And by the looks of this room, I was most definitely in the past.

Fortunately, this man—Nathan—had given me cover that

would allow me the time to figure out to get back to my own time.

However, the downside was that I needed to offer him an explanation. He was more like his aunt than he probably wanted to admit.

"What do you suggest?" I asked.

"The easiest thing would be to say you're my sister's friend," he said. "but that would involve bringing my sister into our ruse."

"You have a sister?"

"Yes. A younger sister."

"Can you trust her?"

He popped a piece of cheese in his mouth and seemed to consider.

"Not a good idea. She's too young."

"I have two sisters."

"Ah. Then you understand."

"Except that I'm the youngest," I said with a little smile.

"Well, then, I suppose you do understand better than I."

"Maybe."

"Were you here for the picnic?" he asked.

"Picnic?"

"No." He leaned back in his chair. "That would be too easy."

The customs in this time period would be different from anything I could think of.

"Since my memory isn't working very well," I said. "I'll have to leave it up to you."

"We'll use that," he said. "And we can teeter on the truth."

"How so?"

"We'll say that your grandfather was bringing you here to visit me and you had an accident. That's all you remember. I'll fill in the rest."

"What will you say?" I refilled my water glass.

"I don't know," he said, but I'm sure I'll think of something."

"I'm sure you will." I added a little smile.

"Do you know where your trunks are?"

"My trunks?"

"Yes. Your clothing."

"Not really." My luggage was in my car, but that would make no difference.

Unable to resist my sudden curiosity, I got up and went to the window and looked out. I should have been able to see my car from here, but, of course, it wasn't there.

Instead, there was an iron hitching post.

Not only was my car gone, but I could see newly plowed fields all the way to the horizon.

I knew this had been farmland a long time ago... a very long time ago. And in my time, there were trees. Pine trees and oak trees. Trees so tall, there was no doubt they had been growing for a hundred years.

See the crops erased any lingering doubt I might have had about whether or not I was in the past.

I was most definitely in the past.

I turned and looked into Nathan's eyes.

He was watching me with obvious curiosity... and something else.

Like me, he was a visitor here.

Perhaps my travel into the past had been more than accidental.

Perhaps I was here to do something. Maybe to change something.

But what? I couldn't even begin to imagine.

16

NATHAN

I left Sophia to meet with my uncle again.

Sophia seemed unconcerned that she was dressed more like a boy than a lady.

Her beautiful long brunette hair was an odd juxtaposition to her boyish clothing. To say that she intrigued me was an understatement.

I was immensely curious about her.

Who was she? How did she get here?

I'd declared to my aunt that I was betrothed to her.

I wasn't sure how my parents would react. On the one hand, they may be furious because I didn't tell them. On the other hand, they might be ecstatic to see me wed. especially since I was thirty years old and hadn't courted anyone.

Until now I hadn't met anyone who piqued my interest enough to marry. Like any normal man I had my dalliances, but that was entirely different from getting married.

I couldn't actually marry this girl, of course. I didn't even know who she was. My parents would insist on knowing who she was before I married her.

They had the Laurent name to protect. Fortunately my

bother Grant took the brunt of the expectations since he was the oldest.

He hadn't shown any interest in getting married either. My parents probably wondered where they had gone wrong.

Three sons and none of them inclined to marry.

I found Uncle Samuel in the stables, brushing one of his horses.

"Eloise told me that you're betrothed," he said.

Apparently, news traveled fast. Barely an hour had passed and already the word was spreading.

"Yes," I said, glancing around. "but no one else knows it."

"Not even your parents?" he asked, brushing the bottom of the horse's hoof.

"Especially not my parents," I said.

My uncle glancing at me, then went back to work on the horse's hoof.

"This one needs to have a shoe replaced," he said.

"Want me to do it?"

He shook his head. "I'll take her in to the blacksmith."

"I don't mind."

"Why don't we take a walk?" he asked. "you can tell me more about this girl."

"Very well," I said. "but I don't want to interrupt you."

"I welcome it," he said. "especially since me knowing more than my wife will drive her crazy."

He would tell her. As he should. I couldn't tell my uncle, or anyone for that matter, anything that I didn't want everyone to know.

That was the thing about living on a farm like this. There wasn't much excitement. So an unknown girl showing up... alone... with no memory... was quite enough. Adding my being betrothed to her only added fuel to the fire.

My uncle put away the brush and took two cigars from his pocket as we left the barn. He handed one to me.

We didn't light them, we merely just enjoyed the scent.

"Should we begin planning a wedding then?" he asked.

It was a natural question. It was, however, something that I hadn't given nearly enough thought.

I knew that I couldn't marry Sophia. But I should have also accounted for my aunt and uncle being social bugs. A wedding was the perfect excuse for them to throw a party.

"Where is Father?" I asked. "I didn't see either him or Mother inside."

"They took a buggy into Natchez. I think they needed to post a letter to your brother."

I blew out a breath. The fates were on my side. I had to figure out what I was going to tell them about Sophia before they heard it from someone else.

17

SOPHIA

Left to my own devices, I slipped from the room and made my way down the hall. Even knowing that I would be better off staying out of sight, I couldn't resist poking around.

The man, Nathan, was different from other men. Maybe it was because he lived in another century.

From the way Eloise was dressed, I would venture to say I was sometime in the 1800s. I wasn't a history buff by any means, but I'd seen enough movies to have a general idea of the way people dressed.

I had to be later in the 1800s, at least according to what I'd learned watching the Bridgertons, but of course, that was England, not America.

Whatever year it was, I'd gone back in time by up to two hundred years. Good heavens. No electricity. No running water.

Grandpa believed that Grandma Vaughn had gone back in time.

I reached the banister and leaned over.

Was Grandma here somewhere?

Two hundred years, though, was a long span of time. Even if she'd come back *here*, she could be any *time.*

The grandfather clock chimed four times. It was four o'clock.

Needing to explore... to see for myself… I went down the stairs and turned left toward the parlor.

Eloise sitting there working on her needlepoint, looked up.

"Come," she said. "Sit with me."

I should have stayed in my room.

Now Eloise was going to have questions for me that I couldn't answer.

"Where are you from?"

"Boston."

"We have relatives in Boston," she said.

"Really?" I didn't know of any of my ancestors being from Boston. But then my father hadn't talked to me about his family and my mother certainly hadn't. I didn't know much about my father's people.

And by the time I started going around Grandpa, I was of the age when I had no interest in such things. I had my own teenage interests. Music. Boys. The usual.

I should have listened to him as an adult. But I'd been too busy with work. Too busy with my own life.

And now it would have benefited me to at least have a working knowledge of the Becquerel family.

"I might know some of your people," she said. "who are you related to."

"Vaughn Becquerel," I said.

Eloise's shocked expression told me that I wasn't very good at this game of pretending to be someone I wasn't.

"Vaughn." She said the name reverently, then seemed to catch herself. "The news of her passing was quite a shock to us all."

I caught my breath. My grandmother had passed in the past as well.

My grandfather had been right then.

And yet…

Even though I'd found her, I was too late.

"So," Eloise said, changing the subject. "How long have you known my nephew?"

"Not very long," I said.

"It's so nice to see him happy." Eloise smiled. "Always such a serious boy. I've never seen him this happy."

I didn't say anything. I didn't know what to say. Whether or not Nathan had been happy before was beyond my ability to know.

"Do you not have anything to wear, Dear?" she asked.

I glanced down at my jeans and Ralph Lauren t-shirt.

"My trunks were lost… I think."

"Then we must find you something suitable to wear." Eloise dropped her hands into her lap.

Grandpa had suggested that people could return from the past. But he'd never said how long they would stay.

If my grandmother was any indication, it was more than just a short visit.

I suppose I should resign myself to staying here, in the past, for longer than a few hours.

I nodded. "That's very kind of you."

And perhaps very necessary to my survival.

18

NATHAN

After spending about an hour talking with Uncle Samuel, I was itchy to get back to the main house.

Uncle Samuel and I hadn't even talked about business. We'd talked about Sophia and when I might want to have a wedding. I had to say that I had never seen this side to my uncle. Once he started talking about how he'd met Eloise and how they'd been married, there was no stopping him.

But he finally realized that it was time to get ready for supper. We walked together across the yard toward the house.

As we passed the window at the stairway landing, I found myself looking up.

Sophia wouldn't be there. She would be in the guest room where I had left her. But it didn't stop me from looking in anticipation of seeing her again.

I told myself I was being ridiculous. Not more than two hours had passed and already I was ready to see her again.

I was like a schoolboy. Yet I had attended an all boy's school. And there had been no ladies at the academy. There had been women, of course, but no one to bring home.

And now I'd declare myself betrothed… to a lady I didn't

even know. And I was pretended that I did.

What had I done?

Uncle Samuel was rattling on about how Aunt Eloise would want to have an outdoor wedding before the weather got too hot. Otherwise, it would be best to wait until fall.

Had they seriously already talked about this? Or was this just standard for them?

This excuse to have a soiree?

My family was more private. It was interesting how that worked. My family would have seemed to be better off living in the country where privacy was a given whereas my uncle would have been better off living in the city where there were always people around.

But I supposed things didn't always work out logically like that.

"Uncle," I said as we walked across the back veranda and went in through the back door. "Will you do something for me?"

"Of course, my boy. What is it?"

"Don't say anything to my parents about Sophia until I've had a chance to explain it to

them."

"Not a problem," he said. "I understand."

"Thank you."

"But you should know that I can't make any promises about your Aunt Eloise."

Well, hell. So much for that.

"Are they returning tonight? Are do you think they'll stay in town at one of the inns?" I asked.

"As far as I know, they're coming back, but they really didn't say."

"I'm going up to check in on Sophia. Then I might ride out to meet them."

"Good idea." Uncle Samuel clapped me on the back. "You're

a good man, Nathan."

Leaving my uncle, I went upstairs and straight to the guest room.

Before I left, perhaps I would procure a proper dress for Sophia to wear. It wouldn't do for her to meet my parents wearing her boy's garb.

I should have asked her how she came to be wearing such clothing to begin with. It didn't, however, seem like an appropriate thing to ask a lady.

I knocked on the thick wooden door.

Hearing no answer, I knocked again.

Then I heard female voice on the other side of the door.

What the—?

I hadn't specifically suggested that Sophia stay hidden away. But she had all but asked me to do just that.

How, then, was it that she had been found?

I held my hand to the wood to knock again, but I heard a familiar voice... Aunt Eloise?

Surely not.

I turned the knob and slowly opened the door.

A quick scan told me that Aunt Eloise was indeed here along with her lady's maid, Abigail.

Sophia stood next to the bed wearing nothing more than a chemise. Abigail stood behind her, tightening the corset with the ties while Sophia held one of the four posters of the bed.

Since Sophia's eyes were closed, she didn't see me.

But I got an excellent view of her bosom straining against the top of the corset.

Suddenly my mouth was dry and I struggled to catch my breath.

The young lady in the tight pants and painted shirt had bloomed right before my eyes.

And I felt the attraction all through my body, the blood pooling right in my center.

19

SOPHIA

I didn't need a corset. I didn't even wear Spanx. But Eloise and her lady's maid, Abigail, insisted that a lady wore a corset whether she needed one or not. Something about a lady's feminine shape.

"Hold still and suck in your stomach" Abigail said as I took a deep breath.

"Do you wear these all day long?" I asked, at my wit's end.

"Of course, Eloise said. "Don't you?"

"No," I said, then backtracked. "Not when I'm home alone."

"What if someone comes to visit?" Abigail asked. "You'd be caught half dressed."

I rolled my eyes.

They had no idea. If they saw me walking around the pool in my bikini, in public, no less, they would pass out.

The door closed and my eyes widened.

"Was someone at the door?" Eloise asked.

"Heavens," Abigail said. "I hope not. What with this child half dressed."

"I'll go see," Eloise said, her skirts rustling as she crossed the room to the door.

I had to admit that Eloise did look elegant in her long gown. But to dress like that every day all day long seemed unfathomable.

"There," Abigail said. "Now we can put on the dress."

What was the point in wearing clothes when one couldn't breathe?

"Can you let it out just a little?" I asked. "I think I'm going to faint." I looked over my shoulder with what I hoped was my most compelling expression.

Abigail muttered something about not being proper, but she released the ribbon enough that I could catch my breath.

"Thank you."

Eloise came back into the room.

"Did you see anyone, Madam?"

Eloise didn't answer. Instead she went to the window and looked outside.

I was left with the formidable Abigail.

"Arms out," she said.

I put my arms out and she dropped a dress over my head. For a moment, I was lost in a hundred yards of soft silver silk.

But Abigail deftly pulled the dress down and straightened the material in quick order.

"This is a good color for you," she said. "not everyone can wear silver like this."

"Whose dress is this?" I asked.

"It belonged to Missus Vaughn Becquerel."

"Vaughn," I said, sucking in a breath.

"Don't you worry though. It might be a little outdated, but it fits you so perfectly no one will notice."

I looked down at the silvery gown, belled out with hoop skirts. I saw nothing in the least different from the one Eloise wore.

"Look in the mirror," Abigail said.

Walking in the dress required a different skill set from wearing jeans and sneakers.

I walked slowly, navigating the heavy gown that swept the floor behind me.

Stopping in front of the full-length mirror, I didn't recognize myself. I looked like a completely different person. The corset kept me straight, whether I wanted to be or not.

This was my grandmother's Vaughn's dress and oddly enough I could see her in it.

Did I look like her?

I had to admit that I felt different. Though how, I wasn't quite sure just yet.

A wagon approached the house. Eloise turned back to the window.

"My sister and her husband are back," she said over her shoulder. "I must speak with them."

And with that comment, she swished out of the room, closing the door behind her.

Dogs howled outside, no doubt in greeting to Eloise's relatives.

20

ELOISE BECQUEREL

Eloise Becquerel's hands shook as she opened the door to her bedroom and went to the desk in her study.

Sophia Becquerel in the guest room wearing the dress that Vaughn had worn to Eloise's wedding.

Eloise had been so happy and in love that she'd barely noticed, and certainly didn't care that Vaughn had stolen the title of most beautiful woman at the wedding and the following reception.

Sophia looked so much like Vaughn. It was as though Vaughn had sprung back to life.

Eloise dropped into her chair, an unladylike motion that she rarely allowed herself.

Pulling open the bottom drawer, she took out the box of letters that had belonged to Vaughn. None of the letters had been mailed.

In fact, Eloise often wondered why Vaughn didn't simply write her thoughts in a journal.

Flipping through the letters, she quickly found the one she was looking for.

It was the last one Vaughn wrote.

Taking the letter, a thick cream-colored piece of paper, she unfolded it and began to read.

Dearest Jonathan,

Someday you will read these letters, though it may not be in my lifetime.

First of all, I want you to know how much I love you. No matter where I find myself in time, I always think of you. You never leave my thoughts, in fact, for more than a few minutes.

It's the oddest thing. Something I think only you could appreciate.

Today I attended my great-grandson's wedding. Only you can know how impossible that sounds.

I've traveled... so much that my timeline is mixed up.

At any rate, it was a lovely wedding.

Someday, if you read this, know that you are in my thoughts.

That great-grandson was Eloise's husband and the wedding was hers.

Vaughn had disappeared shortly after that. Though no one knew where she was, everyone assumed that she had passed away.

She had been in marital bliss and had not paid so much attention to the situation as she might have otherwise.

It was a mystery, though, that she had pondered from time to time.

The one thing that had never left her thoughts was just how beautiful and young-looking Vaughn had been.

Yet... she had been older.

That was the thing about youth. Everyone over twenty-five looked equally old. It hadn't occurred to her until years later that Vaughn had been much too young to be her husband's great-grandmother.

Something was amiss.

Something she could not explain.

And yet now that she had seen Sophia, she was more convinced than ever that something wasn't right.

Maybe it was a maternal instinct, but she felt the need to protect Sophia.

Something about her. Maybe it was the way she looked. Maybe it was something in her eyes.

Whatever it was, she knew what she had to do.

She also knew that it would not be a popular decision.

Eloise, however, was of an age when the opinions of others no longer mattered.

Besides… she had seen something like this before.

21

NATHAN

My parents had returned from Natchez before I had the chance to intercept them.

They had no more than ridden up when Aunt Eloise summoned them to the parlor.

I went into my uncle's study and sat at the desk I'd been using earlier. I tried to concentrate on my paperwork, but I kept thinking about Sophia.

I'd thought she was beautiful the first time I'd seen her. But seeing her wearing nothing more than a chemise had done something to my brain.

Her bosom had swelled against the top of the chemise… her long lightly curled hair framed her face and fell around her shoulders.

I dipped the quill into the ink and signed my name on one of the papers.

"Sir?" Villars, the butler, stood in the doorway, tall and straight. As usual, he wore a somber expression.

"What is it Villars?" My gut swirled with dread. My Aunt Eloise knew too much. And now she was bringing my parents into it. I hadn't even had the opportunity to tell them that I had decided to marry.

Oddly enough, the more I thought about marrying Sophia, the more I liked the idea.

And heavens, I had only spoken to her one time.

Again, she had done something to my brain.

"Your presence is requested in the parlor."

"Great." I set the quill aside and wiped my fingers on a cloth.

"Shall I tell them you're on your way, Sir?" Villars asked.

"Of course, Villars," I said. "Thank you."

"My pleasure."

After Villars left, I scrubbed a hand over my chin and put away my ink. Again.

I walked toward the parlor like a man walking to the gallows.

Being summoned to my parents was bad enough, but Aunt Eloise? She was the most frightening woman I knew.

I had no reason to think that way. She'd never actually done anything to me.

I had, however, heard horror stories from my cousins about her strictness. Whether those tales were true or not I had no way of knowing.

"Come in," Father said as I stepped through the door into the parlor. Father stood in front of the cold fireplace.

Mother and Aunt Eloise sat on the sofa, a little teapot and cups on a tray on the table in front of them.

It looked like they were having a tea party. What could they possibly want from me?

The French doors stood open, letting in a light breeze that smelled like the freshly bloomed spring flowers outside.

"To what do I owe this pleasure?" I asked, wanting to be anywhere but here.

Aunt Eloise and Mother exchanged a glance.

"Eloise has just informed us of your intentions to marry," Mother said.

"That can only mean one thing," Aunt Eloise added, picking up her teacup and taking a little sip.

"Is it true?" Mother asked.

"I'm afraid I don't know what you're referring to."

Father stepped forward. "Have you compromised the young lady?"

"What? No."

I had never been so taken aback.

While other men might frequent brothels, I had an impeccable reputation. I stayed out of brothels, I didn't gamble, and I paid my debts.

What more could anyone expect of a man my age?

Indeed, unlike ladies, society put no pressure on me to marry, especially since I wasn't the oldest son.

"Then. What is the urgency?" Mother asked.

"I never said—" Urgency? Where had that come from?

"The wedding needs to take place as soon as possible," Aunt Eloise said.

"Mother?" Mother looked away.

"Father?" Father shrugged and took a cigar from his pocket.

"What do you know of this girl?" Father asked.

"As I told you," Aunt Eloise said. "She's a Becquerel."

"Then she is more than suitable," Mother said.

Perhaps my feeling of being summoned to the gallows had been an understatement.

"I do want to marry her," I said. "but there is no urgency. Whoever told y—"

"It's best to get married now," Aunt Eloise said. "in the spring. Before it gets too hot to have a wedding."

How could the heat possibly have anything to do with whether or not a man got married?

"There's been a grave misunderstanding," I said.

"Nathan," Father said. "Let's take a walk."

Yes. A walk was an excellent idea.

Anything to get me away from so many pairs of eyes asking me for an explanation I couldn't provide.

22

SOPHIA

A young girl named Rose pulled and tugged on my hair. She deftly wrapped ribbons around strands and somehow pulled my hair on top of my head, leaving just enough strands down that I didn't look severe.

"Are we going to some kind of event?" I asked.

"Event?"

"Yes," I said. "It seems you're going to a lot of trouble with my hair."

Maybe they were going to take me into town and set me out on the street.

"No ma'am. We're just going to dinner."

"Do we have some special guests coming for dinner?"

"Oh no. Just dinner with the family."

Alarm bells shot through me.

Why would I be having dinner with the family?

"To celebrate your engagement, ma'am," she said.

"Right."

My engagement.

Nathan had told his aunt that we were to be married.

I hadn't thought about the ramifications of that at the time.

I had only been thinking about buying some time for me to find my way back to my own time.

"There," Rose said, holding up a small gold handled mirror. "You look lovely."

I recognized myself even less than I had when I'd first looked at myself wearing the silver dress.

I had to admit that it was growing on me. I felt more feminine than I had ever imagined.

Although I readily recognized that the space a person occupied determined how they felt and even made them who they were, I hadn't given much thought to how clothing could do the very same thing.

If nothing else, I'd already learned something from this experience.

When I got back to my time, I was going to change the way I dressed. I was going to start wearing skirts and maybe dresses. At least some of the time anyway.

Maybe not all the time.

Maybe not when I was out on construction sites.

At any rate, I would certainly be more aware of how dress affected a person's state of mind. Much like their space did.

Leaving my room, I went out into the hallway and headed toward the stairway.

I was going to have dinner with my fiancé's family.

Placing a hand on my stomach, I fought off a flutter of butterflies.

A fiancé I didn't even know.

But right now nothing was familiar to me.

I reached the top of the stairs and carefully navigated my way down. It was not easy achievement with so many yards of material.

After walking past the landing, I stopped halfway down the second flight.

Eloise and a woman I didn't recognize sat in the parlor,

their heads bent together in conversation. They both wore dresses much like mine. Eloise wore blue and the other woman wore green.

Eloise saw me and directed the other woman's attention in my direction.

The two of them watched me as I stood there, wondering what I was supposed to do.

I had no choice, really, except to join them.

But just as the grandfather clock began to chime the hour, the front door opened and Nathan stepped inside.

He froze, staring up at me.

My breath caught in my throat at the way he looked at me.

He looked at me as though I was the most beautiful woman he had ever seen.

And I was charmed by his handsomeness.

His eyes left mine for barely an instant as he bowed.

I glanced toward the two women in the foyer. Though they still watched me, they couldn't see Nathan from their vantage point.

Determined to join Nathan and get out of their sight, I dashed—however carefully—down few remaining steps.

But just as I reached the bottom of the stairs, I realized that Nathan was no longer there.

And then I heard the clear and unmistakable sound of the Weather Channel on the television.

I froze, with one foot on the floor, the other on the last step.

I was no longer in the past.

23

NATHAN

My feet were frozen to the floor.

Sophia had vanished into thin air.

I had looked down for about half a second, maybe less. Not nearly enough time for her to walk away.

But yet she was no longer on the stairs.

Forcing my feet to move, I went to where she stood on the stairway.

Though she had vanished, I almost felt like I could sense her. That was nonsense, of course.

But where had she gone?

Then I saw Aunt Eloise and Mother. Gaping at me from the parlor.

Looking away, I pressed a hand against my forehead.

What had just happened?

Mother and Aunt Eloise had seen Sophia vanish, too.

"Nathan." It was Aunt Eloise.

They would be looking to me for answers. But I didn't have one.

"Come here."

I went to the parlor door and looked at them.

Aunt Eloise was standing now, but Mother was still seated and she looked rather pale.

"What happened?" Mother asked.

"I need both of you to sit down," Aunt Eloise said.

"Do you have an explanation?" I asked. How could Aunt Eloise possibly look so calm? Maybe she hadn't seen Sophia vanish. Maybe she'd somehow missed it.

But I sat down anyway. And not a minute too late.

A grown man, of course, would never admit that he had grown weak in the knees even over something so… baffling.

"Are you alright, Mother?" I asked.

"Quite," she said with a tight smile. "I'm sure there's a good explanation."

I nodded.

Aunt Eloise sat down again, across from us and clasped her hands together in her lap. A harbinger of trouble to come, no doubt, but I didn't have the energy to worry about her so much right now.

I steadied my own hand on my knees and forced myself to focus on my aunt.

"As I said, you'll need to marry her sooner rather than later." Aunt Eloise kept her gaze on mine.

I swept my hand back toward the stairway.

"How am I to marry someone who isn't there?"

"Exactly," Aunt Eloise said.

"What do you know of her?" I asked. "And her… disappearance?"

"I don't know anything," Aunt Eloise said. "Not for certain. But… I do have thoughts."

"Do share." I straightened my jacket and waited.

Aunt Eloise glanced at Mother.

"I think she is from the future."

I would have been no more shocked if Aunt Eloise had announced that she… or Sophia was from the moon.

"Why would you say such a thing?"

Aunt Eloise looked at me as though I were daft.

"You saw the way she was dressed?"

"I did," I said, remembering the tight boy's pants and the white shirt with the painting on it.

"I've seen something like that before."

"Have you traveled through time Eloise?" Mother asked.

"Certainly not."

"Then you mustn't say such things about Nathan's betrothed."

"Very well," Aunt Eloise said. "But not saying it doesn't make it so."

Aunt Eloise was oh so very right.

It was as good an explanation as any as to why Sophia had vanished into thin air.

24

SOPHIA

The silver dress billowing around me, I sat on the stairs.

My head buzzed. I closed my eyes and just let my mind go blank.

I *had* been in the past.

Just as sure as the world was round, I had been in the past.

Nathan.

I had vanished right in front of not only Nathan, but also Eloise and another woman.

What must they be thinking?

I shook my head. It made no difference. I had been there, but it had only been for a few hours.

I could leave now. I could get away from this house.

This spell that sent people back in time.

My hands trembling, I stood up and went back upstairs.

As I approached the landing, I heard Grandpa's voice. He was on the phone again.

Heavens. Surely he hadn't been on the phone all this time.

I went to the door to his bedroom study.

He was still pacing, phone to his ear.

"I'll have to call you back," he said and lowered the phone.

I swallowed. His expression frightening me.

"Sophia," he said, his voice rough.

"Grandpa… I…" I couldn't finish the sentence. I couldn't say it out loud.

He came forward. Took my hand and led me to the little sofa in his study.

I sat and shoved my dress aside enough for him to sit next to me.

"Your phone call lasted a long time," I said, my own voice rough.

"You were just here," he said. "not ten minutes ago."

I stared blankly at him.

"Ten… minutes?"

"Yes. You came to the door and I held up a finger."

I nodded.

"You did. But…" The sun was still streaming through the windows. "It was several hours ago." I swept a hand over my dress. "I…"

My eyes welling with tears, I looked at my Grandpa.

"You were only gone for no more than ten minutes," he said. "What happened?"

He lightly touched a strand of my hair.

"You look so much like your Grandmother."

"Grandpa. I think I went back in time."

He nodded. "So it seems."

"How?" I searched his eyes. Looking for answers he didn't have. No one had.

"Actually not so much *how* as *why*."

"Why…" I breathed.

"Grandpa scrubbed his hands over his cheeks and stared into space.

"Did you meet anyone?" he asked.

Nathan's image shot through my mind. But by anyone I knew he meant Grandma.

I shook my head. I'd learned something about Grandma.

But I didn't have the heart to tell him.

25

NATHAN

The night air smelled like a combination of magnolia blossoms and fine Virginian cigar smoke.

Moonlight streamed across the lawn, glistening on the lingering raindrops from the rain and lightning bugs blinked near the line of oak trees.

The sound of frogs croaking drifted from the river and a coyote howled somewhere in the distance.

It was a peaceful evening overall. Peaceful in contrast to the turmoil I felt inside.

Sitting on the balcony outside the guest room where I'd put Sophia, I put one foot on the railing and inhaled the smoky and sweet cigar smoke.

The deep scent of a good cigar normally settled my nerves, but nothing could settle me tonight. I could still taste a hint of the whiskey I'd drank before coming upstairs.

This day had been one of the most bizarre and disturbing I'd ever had in my thirty years.

I'd found the girl I wanted to marry, then she had vanished into thin air.

I would have questioned my sanity if both my Mother and Aunt Eloise hadn't also seen her vanish. My mother was disturbed, perhaps as much as I was, but my Aunt Eloise was not.

She hadn't said it in so many words, but I got the impression that she truly believed that Sophia was from the future and if I had married Sophia she would still be here.

That was beyond me.

Just trying to wrap my head around it made my head hurt.

Wherever she was from, now or the future… New Orleans or Boston… did not change the way I felt about her.

I had never been so certain about anything as I was that I wanted to marry her.

Love wasn't supposed to make sense. I truly believed that love was one of those things that needed no explanation.

And any man who tried to explain it had never experienced it.

Finding her merely strengthened my commitment to establishing my textile mill here. In the northern part of the state.

Wild horses couldn't pull me from here now.

I was committed to going through with my factory. New Orleans had seen the last of me.

I'd talk to my uncle. Settle on a place to start building a house of my own.

In the meantime, I would live here. In the main house. If living here became a problem, I would move out to the garçonnière since I'd seen Sophia there, too.

I'd talk to my uncle. I'd even talk more with my formidable aunt when my mother wasn't around. I would do whatever I had to do to learn more about this time travel. Someone had to know how to explain it.

All I wanted to know was how to make it happen again.

Was there anything I could do to bring Sophia back to me?

Whatever it was, I would do it.

I would do whatever it took to be with the love of my life.

26

SOPHIA

I carefully folded the silver dress and tucked it in my closet. A closet that wasn't there in the past.

It was interesting how the original house had no closets and no bathrooms. Just bedrooms.

Even the kitchen was outside, but that made some sense because if the kitchen caught on fire, the house wouldn't be part of it.

Not having bathrooms or electricity would have made building the house a lot simpler. Overall the house was a simple design.

But over the years everything had been added. Electricity. Air conditioning and heating. Plumbing. Adding it after the fact was quite an achievement.

Probably more so than building the house to begin with.

I'd changed my mind about leaving today. The sense of urgency had passed.

Besides, all that time travel had left me exhausted.

I sat on a stool in the closet and stared blankly at the dress.

I'd felt like Cinderella walking down the stairs in this ball gown.

But my carriage had turned back to a pumpkin *before* the ball. What was up with that?

Now I was back in my world, but I still had both my shoes.

Instead of a slipper, I'd left behind a pair of blue jeans and a white t-shirt—my favorite new t-shirt—a Ralph Lauren logo shirt. It had been a present from my younger sister.

There was nothing I could do about it.

I had their dress… supposedly my grandmother's dress and they had my clothes.

They also had Nathan. Was something wrong with me that I was crushing on a guy who lived hundreds of years ago?

If I could go back to him, would I?

Shaking my head, I left the bedroom and went downstairs for a bottle of water.

I was too restless to sleep anyway.

When I got to the kitchen, Grandpa was sitting at the breakfast table. He rested his chin on his hand, staring into space.

"Are you okay Grandpa?"

"I'm fine," he said. "Just couldn't sleep."

"Me either."

I took a bottle of water from the refrigerator and sat down across from him.

"When you were back there?" he asked. "Do you know what year it was?"

"No. Would you like some water? Or some warm milk?" I was trying to distract him from talking about me going to the past.

"No. No," he said, straightening. "I'm okay."

I drank some water.

"Sophia," he said. "When you were back there… in the past… did you hear anything about your grandmother?"

People often described me as honest. In this moment I now knew what it meant to be honest to a fault

I couldn't lie to my grandfather as much as I wanted to.

"They spoke of her, yes."

"What did they say?" His face brightened.

I shook my head and looked away.

"I was too late," I said.

"I understand." He nodded slowly, his eyes hooded.

"I'm so sorry." I reached over and put a hand over his.

"It's okay," he said, but his eyes were watery. "I'm just happy she was there and hadn't been forgotten."

"Not forgotten at all. In fact, they told me that silver dress had belonged to her."

"I can see that. It fit you perfectly."

"It did, didn't it?" I toyed with the cap of my water bottle. "Grandpa?"

"What's bothering you Sophia?"

I couldn't answer him because I honestly didn't know how to say it. Not out loud. Not even to myself.

"It's nothing," I said.

Maybe I wasn't so honest after all.

27

NATHAN

Two years later

I ran my iron plane over the arm of the rocker, smoothing off the rough edges.

My back porch overlooked the Mississippi River and gave me a nice breeze.

After building myself what I considered a mid-size plantation home, I had discovered that I had a knack for carpentry, of all things.

After my family returned to New Orleans, I'd stayed on at my cousins' house. After the sweltering summer heat abated, I had gotten to work in earnest.

I had made a two-prong attack on my future. The textile mill and the house.

Everyone in Natchez thought I was daft for building a mill.

Just send your crops up north like we always do.

The north has resources we don't.

And the more they talked, the more convinced I was that I was right. How was it they could not seem to understand that they were digging themselves into a deeper and deeper hole?

I was no prophet by any means, but I understood business and I could see that being too reliant on another part of the country to meet our basic needs was a recipe for disaster. Not now. It could be a century from now, but one day it would come back to bite us in the butt.

I'd had help building the framework of the house, the roof, and the floors, but the rest of the finishing out, I'd done myself.

I'd taken my time. Carefully choosing my wood. Doing it my way. I was in no hurry.

I wasn't going anywhere.

After talking to a lot of people, I'd learned that I took after my Uncle Nathaniel. Uncle Nathaniel had fallen in love with Vaughn Dupree.

I'd taking little bits of information from everyone and pieced together the story.

Vaughn was a young lady from France who had traveled to America to marry a stranger. She had not only endured what was no doubt an arduous journey at a tender young age, but she had nearly lost her life when her traveling party had been set upon by Indians during a raging thunderstorm.

One of the Indians, however, had saved her life by casting a spell upon her. The spell had worked by sending her through time.

That's where Uncle Nathaniel had found her. Soaking wet on a beautiful sunny day.

From what I'd gathered, it was love at first sight.

Vaughn, however, had been unable to control the time travel. She would be here for a while, then without warning, she would vanish into another time.

Although I could only imagine that it was hell on both her and Nathaniel, I took solace in the knowledge that I wasn't alone.

I'd chosen a lovely white oak to make the rocker from. It

was the same wood I'd used to make bookcases in both my study and the library.

One of the next things I would do was to send off for books. I'd fill the library with books. I wanted my children to have access to lots and lots of books to read.

I'd send for a piano so my daughters could learn piano. They would be accomplished in music, reading, and languages. I'd hire the best tutors.

I had so many plans in mind and I was in the process of getting everything lined out.

When I wasn't preparing my home, I was over at the —my —textile mill overseeing the construction of it.

I'd hired some good people to build it and it was time to start hiring people to work it. Two different sets of help.

It was a fifteen-minute brisk walk from here to anywhere. What I thought of as the main Becquerel house... the stable where I kept Firefly... and the mill.

I was doing well for myself.

There was just one fly in my ointment. One thing I was missing.

I was missing Sophia.

Just as my Uncle Nathaniel had waited for Vaughn, I would wait for Sophia.

I would wait as long as it took even if it took an eternity.

There would never be another woman for me.

My family and acquaintances thought I was insane.

But it paid off. They left me alone.

No doting mothers thrust their daughters upon me. At first I'd been invited to social event after social event.

But after decline after decline, the invitations had eventually stopped.

I liked it that way.

They called me a hermit.

And they just might be right.

Sitting back on my heels, I looked across toward the river.

One day I would see her again.

And that would be the day I would marry her.

One version of the legend held that marriage could help keep her here. Another held that true love was the key.

Whichever it was made no difference to me, for they were one and same.

I wanted to both love her and marry her.

Using a cloth to dust off the chair, I admired my work. Not bad.

Perhaps I could sell these as boutique, limited pieces of furniture.

The busier I kept myself, the less energy I had to think about Sophia.

If she didn't manage to come back soon, I was going to risk being far too prolific in my endeavors.

In the meantime, though… she visited me in my dreams.

And those dreamtime visits made all the difference.

28

SOPHIA

I stepped out onto the back veranda and took a deep breath.

Grandpa had been spending a lot of time in his flower garden and the brightly colored blossoms provided ample evidence of his efforts.

The way he had blended the colors together couldn't have been more lovely even if they'd been painted on canvas by an artist.

Somehow he'd blended a few feet of white flowers into yellow and then into blue. A live work of art that smelled like a mixture of gardenias and daffodils. I didn't even pretend to know what the blue flowers were.

It had been one year since I'd been back here.

I'd thrown myself into my new job in Boston and hadn't looked up. But after a year of going full speed ahead, my boss had insisted that I take a vacation. He knew I had family in Mississippi and he knew I hadn't visited in over a year.

So here I was.

I'd spoken to Grandpa several times on the phone over the

past year and we'd exchanged a few short emails. Neither one of us had said anything about the time travel.

I supposed out of sight, out of mind was one way of dealing with such mysterious matters.

But now that I was here, I could hardly think of anything else.

Thoughts of Nathan had slipped into my mind when I was deep at work on a project and the evening sun left deepening shadows or when I stood in the shower, my mind vulnerable from sleep and hot water.

I'd thought of him when I walked through the historical Boston Common and wondered if he had ever gone there.

I had not dated anyone, nor had I even given dating more than a passing thought.

People called me driven and focused.

Even though we were close, I rarely even talked to my sisters. I think I was afraid that they would ask me something I couldn't answer or question me about why I was so distant.

I didn't trust myself to keep what had happened to me from them.

And at the same time, I couldn't bring myself to tell them. It was bad enough that Grandpa knew.

I considered myself to be grounded and level-heading. Traveling through time did not mesh with my own perception of myself.

I went back inside and brought the silver dress from the closet.

Stretching it out on the bed, I ran my hand along the soft silk.

I wondered what Nathan was doing now. How had he and his aunt explained me to the other woman?

They were the only two people I had seen other than that woman.

What would happen if I put the dress on again?

Would I go back in time again? Or was there something else that triggered it?

Grandpa insisted that it had something to do with this location. This was where the spell had happened… the rip in time.

No matter. If I didn't go now, I was going to be late meeting my father at the construction site. My father hated for people to be late. Probably more than he hated anything else.

Leaving the dress on the bed, I grabbed my purse, draped it over my head, and headed out.

Grandpa was waiting for me downstairs.

29

NATHAN

I strolled along the path from my house to the main house. Since the day had been warm, I hadn't brought a cloak, but now there was a chill in the air.

A chill and swirls of mist forming along the pathway.

The moon was already full and bright.

It had been a good day and hopefully a good night would follow.

As I approached the fork in the path, one leading to the garçonnière, the other leading to the main house, a dog yelped and whined.

The Becquerels had a number of hound dogs and, although I hadn't seen him today, one of dogs named Biscuit, had become a good companion to me.

Concerned about what happened to one of the dogs, I veered right toward the garçonnière.

Tonight it was quiet. No piano music spilling from the cottage. No laughter.

My cousins were attending one of the early spring balls. Things I didn't concern myself with.

It only took a few minutes for me to reach the garçonnière.

The dog, Biscuit, ran up to greet me, sloppily licking my hands. He was a big dog. More like a small horse, really.

"Come on, Biscuit," I said. "let's find our way home and get some sleep."

But instead of following me like he usually did, Biscuit sat down.

"What is it, Boy?"

Biscuit got up and, watching me over shoulder, headed toward the door to the garçonnière.

Befuddled, I followed.

Biscuit scratched at the door and whined softly.

I looked around, but saw no obvious reason for Biscuit's odd behavior.

He barked once and looked back at me.

"Okay," I said with a little laugh.

I'd never had a dog ask for anything more than food.

Curious, I complied.

The door had been left unlocked. That wasn't particularly unusual. Unlike in New Orleans, people often left their doors unlocked even if they did often lock up their food and supplies.

I pushed the door open for Biscuit to walk through, but he sat down again and refused to moved.

"If you aren't going in, then why should I?"

Fortunately, Biscuit did not answer me.

Never one to show fear, I stepped inside the house.

For what couldn't have been more than a moment, I would go to my grave believing I that had smelled sawdust. And I also saw moonlight streaming through the walls.

Moonlight did not stream through walls. Perhaps it would stream through a house that had merely been framed up, but not once the walls were up.

It must have been a trick of the moonlight, of course.

When I heard voices, a chill skittered down my spine.

I turned my gaze toward the fireplace and saw two men, one older than the other. Then I saw a young lady.

Since she had her back to me, I only know she was a young lady by the long hair flowing down her back.

She was dressed in boy's pants…

My heart flipped over on itself.

Then as though she had sensed me watching her, she turned and looked over her shoulder.

It was her.

It was Sophia.

And even though she looked, I was fairly certain she didn't see me.

Mon Dieu.

She was even more beautiful than I remembered. And I remembered her well.

My initial thought that she had come back to me was immediately chased by the realization that I was mistaken.

She hadn't come to me.

I had gone to her.

30

SOPHIA

Apparently it had been a rainy year. More so than expected.

Hardly any construction had been done at all on my father's house. I was secretly pleased. If I had been here, things would have been different.

I got things done in Boston, for God's sake. In the winter. But it wasn't polite to gloat.

In so many ways, I felt like I'd made a mistake by leaving here and going to Boston instead of seeing this project through.

But Grandpa had said something to me that had frightened me at the time.

You may not come back, he'd told me. Ever.

I hadn't wanted to give up my life.

"What do you think?" Father asked.

My father was wearing civilian clothes—jeans and a button-down shirt… the closest he ever came to casual. Yet he still carried himself like a general.

Asking for my opinion was something unusual for him. Very unusual.

Something he never did.

"I think it's a bit behind schedule."

Grandpa grinned and I caught a glimpse of a smile cross my father's eyes before he nodded.

"Agreed," he said. "We're already a year behind. Do you think you can take over and catch it up?"

"What? Father… I." I swept a glance over my shoulder, around the construction area. Since it was Saturday, the workers weren't here today.

Well working on the weekends would be the first step I'd take in getting things set right.

"I have a job."

"I know you do," Father said. "I just fired the foreman." He raised a hand in the air. "Fired everybody."

Grandpa and I just gaped at while his words sank in.

"Surely you jest," Grandpa said, scratching his chin. "You had some good workers."

"I didn't fire the construction workers. Just everyone else." He locked his gaze on mine. That gaze that put fear in men's hearts. "I'll pay you double what you're making now at the job in Boston to move back here and finish this job."

No. No. Absolutely not.

"But… Father. What would I do after I finished this house? I'd be jobless."

"You'll start your own company. I'll give you the money."

"I… um. Shouldn't you ask your new wife?"

Father waved a hand. "Trichell has her own money. She doesn't concern herself about what I do with mine.

Father was not the kind of man anyone said no to. But he was asking the impossible.

Fortunately Grandpa came to my rescue.

"She's here for a two-week vacation. Let her have time to think about it. You can give her more details about what you're asking. If she's ready, she can make her decision then."

Grandpa Jonathan was, as always, the voice of reason.

Father looked at me questioningly.

"Do we have a deal?" he asked.

With a quick glance at Grandpa, I shrugged. "Sure."

"It's a deal then," he said, holding out a hand.

I shook hands with my father for a deal I never would have imagined.

I'd actually planned on visiting my younger sister and possibly even my older sister, but instead, it looked like I was going to be working.

31

NATHAN

Just as quickly as Sophia had appeared, she had vanished.

I looked toward the door where Biscuit sat waiting patiently… looking at me with big brown eyes that seemed to say *I told you I wasn't going in there.*

What was the meaning of this? Of giving me a teasing glimpse of Sophia after I'd waited and watched for her for an entire year.

I left the garçonnière, suddenly feeling like an intruder, and walked back along the path leading to the main house, Biscuit serving as my escort.

Somehow, during the time I was in my cousin's garçonnière seeing shadowy images of a girl who wasn't there—couldn't be there, darkness had fallen.

The massive oak trees diffused any moonlight that might have lit my way, leaving me to make my way in darkness.

I knew the way, of course. I had walked it many times and didn't need either sunlight or moonlight to make my way.

Besides, I could see light from the house up ahead. I would be there momentarily.

I felt a dizzy.

If I had seen Sophia in what looked like her world, did that mean I had traveled through time?

That wasn't supposed to happen... was it?

As I came out from beneath the shadow of the oak trees, moonlight spilled around me.

I walked along the stone pathway through my aunt's flower garden, stopping to sit on a wrought iron bench surrounded by fragrant magnolia blooms.

Biscuit stretched out on the ground beside me.

In a way I was encouraged.

Time, it seemed, had not forgotten about us.

Had that glimpse of her merely been some kind of reminder that she was out there? Not that I had needed it. I hadn't wavered in my determination to wait for her.

The scent of cigar smoke wafting from the veranda told me that my cousins were home.

I wasn't in the mood for hearing about their escapades. I wanted to slip into my room and climb into bed where I could savor and replay the memory of what I'd seen.

I gave Biscuit a quick pat the head and changed direction.

I'd slip around to the front of the house and go in through the front door.

Biscuit stood up when I did, but apparently he'd gone as far as he was willing tonight.

Sitting on his haunches, he watched me walk off the path through my aunt's flowers.

He was probably a lot smarter than I was when it came right down to it.

No one wanted to face Aunt Eloise's wrath when it came to her flowers.

I was almost through the flowers and safely on the other side of the garden when a flash of hazy moonlight blinded me.

I stopped where I stood, frozen.

The piano music that followed was unexpected. It was a sweet, romantic waltz. My cousin would certainly not come back from a night of dancing and socializing only sit down at the piano.

That would be most unusual.

In fact… now that I looked, I could see through the downstairs window.

There was no one sitting at the piano.

Yet… the music played.

32

SOPHIA

It had been a long day.

The meeting with Father at the construction site and his most unexpected proposal that I not only work for him as I was doing last year, but that work as the one in charge. And on top of that, he was willing bankroll me into starting my own business.

I certainly dreamed of doing that… someday.

Right now I had so many irons in the fire… in Boston… that even taking two weeks seemed impossible.

I stayed behind, taking some time to walk through the house just as I had done last year. Only this year I saw nothing unexplainable.

I was disappointed. There. I could admit it to myself.

And then there was dinner with my Father and Grandfather. The drive into town and back had been painful. I never imagined that I knew much about my father growing up, but now I knew even less about him. We had nothing in common. I couldn't talk to him about Mother, of course. And I knew nothing of his new wife.

Going to the window, I stared out at Grandpa's gardens, the

flowers glistening in the moonlight, the steady tick tick of the sprinklers shooting water over them.

A beautiful night.

My thoughts wandered around aimlessly until they found their way to Nathan.

Thinking about Nathan always brought joy to my heart. At least until I got to the part where we lived in different centuries.

Then I heard music. It was so soft and distant at first, that I thought I imagined it. Then it slowly grew louder.

I was still dressed, so I left my room and headed toward the stairs, following the music. It sounded like classical piano music. Something someone would sit at a piano and play.

I had taken lessons for about a year, but I hadn't practiced, so my parents had given up and let me focus on participating in the math club.

I went down the stairs quickly, barely daring to look to my left, afraid of what… who I might see.

But everything seemed normal. Everything except the music.

It seemed like it was coming more from the back of the house than the front, so I went around to the back and went out the back door.

The scent of flowers mixed with the scent of… cigar smoke.

Grandpa didn't smoke cigars and I was fairly certain my father didn't either.

Besides, they had both gone up to bed.

Now that I stood outside, the music didn't seem to be coming from anywhere.

It was just there.

Maybe it was all in my head.

I started to turn around… to go back inside, but I saw a flash of hazy moonlight twinkling among the flowers.

Curious, I went down the stairs and odder still, the piano music stayed with the house.

Well, that was a relief.

It was rather disconcerting to think that it had all been in my head.

As I walked slowly toward Grandpa's daffodils and magnolia flowers, I slowed, squinting into the glistening moonlight that seemed concentrated there in one particular spot.

As I reached the area, I saw that it was more like mist. It looked thick from a distance, but up close it was hardly noticeable.

Lightning bugs left the flowers and headed off to do whatever lightning bugs did.

One landed on my hand and I smiled in awe.

It sat there, winking at me.

"Sophia?"

My head jerked up. And there, standing right in front of me was… Nathan.

33

NATHAN

My feet were frozen to the ground as the mist swirled around me sweeping lightning bugs skyward.

I merely blinked and there she was.

Sophia.

She was smiling. A lightning bug sitting on her hand.

I swallowed the emotion that overwhelmed me and took a step forward.

If she was really there, I wanted to touch her. To feel her.

She, too, took a step forward and we were standing merely inches apart.

She looked up at me with her beautiful green eyes, framed with long thick lashes, her mouth parted ever so slightly. Her breathing was shallow as though she had just run a long distance. And I felt much the same way.

She was holding her hand up as the lightning bug sat there blinking. I had never seen a lightning bug sit still on purpose.

"I can't..." I held up a hand, my palm out, unable to get my thoughts formed into words. "Are you real?"

"I'm real," she said, raising her other hand in front of mine.

We stood there with our hands held up as though we looked through a window at each other, unable to actually touch.

But it wasn't enough. Would never be enough.

I wanted to actually touch her.

To know that she was real.

"As am I," I said, searching her eyes.

Then unable to stop myself, I pressed my hand forward, clasping her fingers in mine.

She was real. She was so very real.

Now that I had touched her, I couldn't get enough.

I pulled her against me, wrapping my arms around her. Her arms went around my waist as she looked up at me.

I had dreamed of this moment. Every night… every day… for over a year.

I had burned for this woman.

And she was in my arms.

I was never letting her go again.

"Sophia," I breathed.

"Nathan."

I lowered my head, my lips crushing against hers.

I felt the kiss all through me, in every nerve of my body.

My fingers tangled in her silky hair. She tasted like honey. Smelled like heaven. Wild flowers and cinnamon.

Sophia was my love.

I pulled back and smiled as I looked into her eyes again.

Her lips were parted as she took shallow breaths. Her eyes hooded.

I swept a finger along her chin and her lips trembled.

"Don't ever leave again."

She shook her head.

"No." Her voice was barely a whisper.

I heard the rain falling before the first drops landed on the top of my head.

Instinctively I covered Sophia's head with mine.

But someone was walking toward us. Their laughter rang out over the music.

Sophia jumped back, leaving my arms.

Only our fingertips barely touched.

But as what sounded like my cousins walked toward us, she turned and her hand slipped from mine before I could stop her.

I took two steps to follow her.

But she had already vanished into the mist.

And the music stopped.

34

SOPHIA

I ran through the mist.

Running from what, I didn't know.

I was overwhelmed. Too overwhelmed to think.

As I ran toward the house, the music stopped.

It just stopped.

And it was raining. Just a few drops at first, but then the rain was coming down in torrents.

No more lightning bugs. No gentle breeze coming off the river.

Instead thunder rumbled in the distance, growing closer as I stepped across the slippery stones that led toward the house.

I forced myself to slow down. To take a breath.

I was already soaked.

Running wasn't going to change that.

Thunder crashed overhead, now.

I should already be at the house.

But the mist was thick and I could barely see.

The rain ran down into my eyes, blinding me.

I stopped, unsuccessfully shielding my eyes with my hands.

Mist swirled around me so that I couldn't see anything more than a few inches in front of me.

A dog howled somewhere in the distance behind me.

I couldn't see the lights from the house. A power outage?

Maybe I'd gotten turned around.

I swirled and tried to decide which way I needed to go.

The dog howled again. Closer.

I heard men's voices drifting from behind me.

I was definitely turned around.

Taking a deep breath, I continued on my way. Following my instinct.

But I quickened my steps.

Coming out from beneath the trees, I caught a glimpse of the house with the next lightning strike.

I blew out a sigh of relief. All was not lost.

My right foot landed on the edge of a slippery stone and I felt myself falling.

I couldn't stop it.

It all happened so fast.

I landed on my arms and my chin crashed against another of the stones.

Someone called my name…maybe… but I couldn't focus.

The mist swirled around me until I felt engulfed by it.

The last thing I remembered before my eyes closed was a wolf sniffing at me.

It turned up its nose and howled.

Just great. I was going to be eaten alive by wolves.

It was poetic justice.

I'd kissed my prince and now I would be eaten alive.

My mind went blank and the lightning flashed and thunder crashed.

35

NATHAN

No.

This could not be happening again.

Ignoring my cousins, I followed Sophia into the mist.

At first I heard her footsteps.

But she was too far ahead of me.

I couldn't see her in the misty moonlight.

Biscuit barked and raced forward, following her also.

And then all I could hear was my cousins' loud voices.

I wanted to yell at them to shut up. But I couldn't see them.

And since they already thought I was a madman, I chose not to add fuel to the fire.

Instead, I rushed forward, toward the house, the way Sophia had gone, Biscuit behind her.

I would find her.

Biscuit howled and I kept going.

Finally I could see the house up ahead. Illuminated by candlelight.

But I saw no sign of Sophia.

None.

Then I saw Biscuit coming back toward me. Reaching me,

he licked my fingers, then kept going, back toward the garçonnière.

The empty expanse of lawn and gardens glowed in the moonlight.

I stopped and slowly turned around, but I already knew she wasn't here.

It was a cruel joke that time played on us.

I could still feel her lips on mine. Her soft body pressed against mine.

I would live on it the rest of my life if I had to.

In the meantime, I would turn over every rock to find her.

I had grown good at waiting.

Seeing her again. Touching her. Kissing her. Had merely added to my resolve.

I'd thought I was in love before.

But now…

Now… oh my…

Now I had her taste… her scent… to add to my memories. My longing.

There was no denying now. Not to anyone.

I didn't care if my cousins thought I was crazy.

Perhaps I was.

I was in love with an apparition.

It was the card I'd drawn.

I wasn't stuck spending my life with some woman I didn't love.

Knowing it could be far worse, I would manage.

I kept walking, knowing… believing that she was here somewhere.

But my cousin, Marvin, intercepted me.

"What are you about?" he asked. Even from here I could smell the alcohol on him.

"Just taking a stroll," I said, not wanting to engage with my cousin.

Marvin elbowed his companion—a man I had not seen before.

"I told you," Marvin said in a loud whisper. "He's daft."

"He doesn't look insane," the other fellow said, peering at me from equally drunken eyes. "He seems quite nice."

Marvin shoved at his friend, the two of them nearly falling down together, catching each other before they hit the ground.

Rolling my eyes, I walked around them. I had no time for such nonsense.

I was looking for the love of my life.

36

SOPHIA

I sat up slowly. My jeans so soaked and heavy I could barely move my legs.

The rain had gone on its way, leaving nothing more than the echo of thunder in its wake.

I didn't know how long I'd been out, but I took my time getting my bearings.

I was outside in the gardens. In fact… I was lying in my grandfather's flower bed.

Oh no.

He was going to be devastated. He loved his flowers.

Brushing gardenia leaves from my palms, I stood up and started walking toward the house.

As I neared the veranda, I smelled cigar smoke.

Cigar smoke?

Grandpa didn't smoke.

Was I back in time then? My heart leapt.

This was something I hadn't dared to want.

But then my hopes crashed back to reality.

It was my father sitting on the veranda.

And he was smoking a cigar.

What new thing was this? My father smoking a cigar?

Maybe he was different being here in the country.

As all these thoughts ran through my head, I walked unsteadily toward him.

I knew the moment my father saw me.

He stood up and tossed his cigar on the ground as he raced down the steps toward me.

"What's happened?" he asked, his long strides reaching me in moments.

He put his hands lightly on my elbows and looked at my face.

"I 'um…" I looked away, trying to think. "I fell down."

"You're hurt," he said.

"No." I shook my head. Not hurt. Lost. But not hurt.

Nathan.

I shifted to look over my shoulder, but Father gently tugged my attention back to him.

"Why are you out here so late?"

"Late?" I'd left the construction site before dark. Hadn't I?

No… I had come home.

I was so confused.

"Why are you drenched?" Father asked.

"The… the storm." I searched his eyes. "The thunderstorm."

"Sophia," he said. "There was no storm."

I swallowed the bubble of hysterical laughter that threatened to bubble up and glanced down at my soaked clothes. My hair, too, was soaked.

"The sprinklers," Father said. "You walked in the sprinklers."

No. I had not walked in the sprinklers.

But Father did not take no for an answer. If he said I walked through the sprinklers and got drenched, then that's how it was going to be.

"You're bleeding," Father said.

I put a hand to my forehead and felt the stickiness of fresh blood.

"We have to get you to the hospital."

"I'm okay," I said.

"You shouldn't be out here at night anyway."

Nonetheless, I didn't need a hospital

I needed Nathan.

37

NATHAN

Later that year

As I walked along the dirt room from what was going to be my textile factory to my house, fallen oak leaves crunched beneath my feet.

I'd worn my long black cloak today to protect myself from the chill in the air.

It had been a long hot summer, but the winter promised to be a cold one. From severely hot to severely cold.

I'd moved into my own place so now I had even more time alone.

More time to think about Sophia.

More time to pace the hall of my own home and walk the grounds of the Becquerel Estate looking for any sign of Sophia.

Although Biscuit had led me to Sophia that night months ago, he'd gone right back to being just a regular dog.

He'd taken up with me, though, even more since then. In fact, he walked at my side right now, his head high, his ears up.

We were quite a pair. Both of us always on alert.

I was always looking for any glimpse of Sophia. Biscuit was looking for whatever dogs looked for. Rabbits maybe.

Or maybe he was looking for Sophia, too.

I'd promised myself that when I saw her again, I wouldn't let her go. I'd had her in my arms. I'd had her in my clutches.

And she had still slipped right out of my hands.

In my darkest moments, my thoughts insisted that she and I weren't meant to be together.

But during most of the time, I dreamed about the day we would be together again.

And we would be together again.

I believed.

As the sun started its dip behind the trees, I took the fork in the road that would lead to my home.

Biscuit barked and looked at me uncertainly.

A woman, wearing a dark cloak similar to mine walked beneath the oak trees toward us.

My heart lodged in my throat.

Was it Sophia?

It was a woman, wearing a long gown, her head covered with the hood.

I stopped and Biscuit stopped, too, sitting down next to me.

He let out a soft, uncertain bark.

The woman stopped just a few feet in front of us and let the hood slide back.

I immediately saw some similarities to Sophia, but marked differences. The most obvious was her age.

It could be Sophia… an older version of her.

No one said time travel had to be linear.

"Hello Nathan," she said.

The woman was definitely not Sophia. Her voice had a different lilt to it. A touch of French, perhaps.

"My name is Vaughn Becquerel."

I inhaled sharply.

I had heard of Vaughn Becquerel.

THE legend. The one who started it all.

"A ghost?" I breathed, my fingers coming to rest on Biscuit's head as though he could keep me grounded… maybe even safe.

"No," she said with a small smile. "I'm not a ghost."

"I don't understand."

Why was she here then? What could she want with me?

"You love Sophia," she said.

"Yes… but… How do you know this?"

She smiled that small smile again.

"I have ways."

"I can only imagine."

"You wait for her," she said. "Much like Nathaniel waited for me."

"You came back to him."

She turned and started walking toward my house.

I fell into step beside her.

"Time has made me different." She looked up at the moon already visible in the sky. "I know things. More than I should."

Alarm shot through me and I froze.

"Has something happened to her? To Sophia?"

"No," Vaughn said, quickly. "Nothing like that."

"Then what?"

She was talking to me for a reason. The sooner I uncovered her true purpose, the better.

I was not one to play games.

I had too much to do.

"I think there's something you have to do," she said.

38

SOPHIA

My father was nothing if not persistent. Persistent and by the book.

I spent the night in the hospital. Head scans. Neurological evaluations.

Then I went back to Grandpa's house with a mild traumatic brain injury diagnosis which I chose to ignore, medication I would not take, and orders to stay off airplanes for ten days which I would disregard.

What I did not tell anyone about was my encounter with Nathan.

Being evaluated for a head injury was one thing. Being evaluated for a mental disorder was another thing entirely and would have kept me in the hospital for an indefinite amount of time.

I wanted to go home. Home being Grandpa's house. And back near Nathan.

While morning turned into afternoon, I paced the bedroom. To the window overlooking Grandpa's garden, to the door, and back again.

The bed was made. The silver dress back in the closet.

Two bottles of water sat next to the bottle of medicine on the nightstand.

I was supposed to be resting. I didn't feel like sitting still for one thing. And even if I did, my brain wasn't in the mood to focus on work.

I wasn't a TV watcher. I read fiction, but, again, my thoughts were too unsettled.

I stopped at the window and looked at the blue flowers that faded into yellow that faded into white.

Right in the middle was a smushed place where I'd fallen down and destroyed the flowers.

I lightly touched the bandage across the middle of my forehead. Everybody was making it out to be something worse than it was.

But that was my father's doing. I'd hardly seen him since I'd left home, and we'd never been close, but he'd gone into full blown take charge General mode.

I paced back to the door.

Back again.

Standing at the window, I pressed one palm against the cool glass.

It reminded me of my encounter last night with Nathan.

We'd stood just like this.

Palm to palm.

A shiver ran through me as I replayed the scene in my head.

Then he'd kissed me.

I closed my eyes.

I wanted to kiss him again.

More than anything right now.

More than I wanted to work.

More than I wanted to return to Boston.

The realization caught me off guard.

What was happening to me?
Maybe I really had damaged something in my brain.
With both hands on the glass now, I made a decision.
Right then and there I decided what I wanted to do.
Whirling around, I went to the closet.

39

NATHAN

It was the night of the Becquerel Autumn Ball.

A beautiful night with moonlight streaming through all the open windows mixing with the light of a hundred oil lamps.

A dozen formally dressed couples seem to float on the lively music from a small orchestra in one corner of the room.

Another dozen people milled about the room. Men and women. Talking. Laughing.

The very type of social event I had managed to avoid for some time.

I straightened my crimson cravat and stepped over the punch table.

The Becquerel ballroom was decked out with flowers of all colors from the gardens. But the colorful flowers had nothing on the lovely dresses the ladies wore.

One young lady… I think her name was Grace… saw me and smiled.

I nodded, then looked away.

Second later she stood at my side.

"Good evening," she said, toying with the dance card at her wrist.

"Good evening."

I busied myself with filling a glass with punch.

Then, as though on second thought, I held it out to Grace.

She smiled as she took it.

Grace was a pretty young lady, but I wasn't interested.

She took a sip of her punch.

"I'm afraid I arrived late and I have a few spaces left on my dance card."

A quick glance told me all the dances on her card were open. And I happened to know that she had actually arrived early.

"You'll have to excuse me," I said.

Suddenly in need of something stronger—much stronger—than punch, I turned on my heel and left her standing there.

I went into the study and closed the door.

Breathing a sigh of relief, I filled a glass with whiskey and drank it down.

I couldn't stay in here long.

I'd just needed to fortify myself against Grace.

You have to go to the Autumn Ball, Vaughn had said.

She'd ignored my protests.

You have to go.

I informed her that I had no interest in courting anyone.

Nathan. I know things.

I know how things are going to happen.

Her words had left me speechless.

You GO to the ball.

And that is where you meet Sophia.

When I'd asked her to explain, she had merely shaken her head, smiled a secret smile, and turned.

I'd called out to her.

Had taken two steps forward to follow her.

Biscuit had uttered one small bark, but he didn't go with me.

Then Vaughn had quite simply vanished.

So here I was.

At the Becquerel Autumn Ball.

Following the mysterious instructions of Vaughn Becquerel.

She had said *you GO to the ball.* Not *you WILL go.*

I'd been a hair's breadth away from not coming tonight.

The thought of my future being already decided had been so very disconcerting.

And I would have stayed away except for one thing.

If there was the remotest chance that Sophia could be here tonight, it was enough to bring me out of my seclusion.

40

SOPHIA

"I've lost my mind."

After stripping down, I pulled the silver ball gown on over my head and fought my way through the yards and yards of silk. Then it just miraculously fell into place.

"Well."

I straightened the skirts and turned this way and that in front of the full-length mirror.

The skirt belled out over the hoop skirt just like it was supposed to.

Going to the dresser, I sat down and ran a brush through my hair.

I would simply have to wear it down. Pulling my hair up into an up-do was something I had never been adept at.

Then there was the matter of the bandage on my forehead.

Carefully pulling a corner loose, I examined my wound.

It wasn't so bad.

A little colorful, but it was healing nicely.

But not yet. I pressed the bandage back down. It was too soon to remove it.

Besides, oddly enough, it reminded me of the kiss in the garden.

Everything reminded me of the kiss in the garden.

I remembered it in vivid detail from the thunder storm to the lightning bug… to the feel of his hands clasped with mine.

The soft firmness of his lips.

I slowly set the brush down.

Had the fall affected my brain?

It was late and Grandpa had gone to bed and my father had left earlier today, so I had the house to myself.

Perhaps I would just stay here in my room.

I slowly stood up and walked back to the window. The belled skirts flowed around me and, just like before when I'd worn the dress, I felt like a princess.

I pressed my hands against the glass.

It was a beautiful clear night. Perhaps I would go back out to the gardens after all.

I thought I imagined it at first, but then I saw a big dog move out from the shadow of the trees.

He sat there at the edge of the trees and looked up at me.

A stray dog perhaps?

I hadn't seen him around before.

But I heard a wolf… perhaps a dog… howling.

My phone chimed with a text message.

I picked it up from the nightstand.

VICTORIA: *Are you ok? Father told me what happened.*

I lowered my phone in exasperation. I'd asked Father not to tell anyone what had happened. I didn't want them worrying.

But Victoria was in her last year of medical school, so it made sense that he would tell her.

The dog had vanished back into the shadows.

ME: *I'm fine.*

If standing in a ball gown from the 1800s was considered fine. Actually, it was far from it.

VICTORIA: *You didn't tell us.*

ME: *Didn't want you to worry.*

And I had some things I needed to figure out for myself.

Like what I was going to do about my crush on a man who lived in the past.

The thing was… I had kissed him BEFORE I fell down and hit my head.

So no matter how much I wanted to, I could not blame my craziness on my fall.

41

NATHAN

By the time I had fortified myself with two glasses of strong whiskey, Grace had found another man to dance with.

Relieved, I nonetheless kept myself on the edge of the festivities.

I wasn't here for them.

I was here for Sophia.

It didn't matter that my logical brain insisted it was all nonsense.

I knew in my core that the kiss I had shared with Sophia had been magical.

It had sealed the deal for me.

A deal I had already made with myself.

The grandfather clock began to chime the hour just as the orchestra took their first break.

The echo of the music was filled with voices and laughter as the guests made their way to the refreshment table.

I slipped out into the foyer and made my way across the hall toward the library.

Aunt Eloise was coming from the dining room.

"Nathan," she said. "I'm so glad you came tonight."

"It was kind of you to ask me." I dipped my head in a quick bow.

"You're always welcome and you know it," she said.

Then she did what every woman did when met with an eligible bachelor at a ball.

"Is there a young lady who has snagged your interest?" she asked, assuming I was looking for a wife.

"Aunt Eloise?" I had to ask because no one had said a single thing about it.

"Yes, Dear?"

"Do you remember Sophia?"

"Who is Sophia?" she asked, her brows creased.

"You don't have to pretend," I said.

"I'm afraid I don't know what you're talking about," she said, then looked past me. "Please excuse me. I believe your uncle is looking for me."

I watched her walk away.

Did she truly not remember Sophia?

Or was she trying to protect me?

The thought that I had imagined Sophia ran through my head again. Maybe I had imagined her.

Since no one had spoken of her to me, it was the only explanation I could come up with.

But Vaughn believed her.

Vaughn. The woman everyone knew had passed away some years ago.

So now I had spoken to two ghosts.

One from the past and one from the future.

I turned on my heel and went into the library. I had no reason to be here.

No real purpose.

I went into the darkened library and sat in one of the armchairs.

The guests were only getting started in their festivities.

But my time here was done.

I would slip out the back and head back to my own home.

It was time to put this nonsense behind me.

When, not if, but when Sophia returned to this time, I would know.

Listening to the ramblings of a ghost predicting that she would be here at a particular ball on a particular night was nonsense.

I'd done my homework. I knew that time travel didn't work like that.

No one could predict how or when it happened. It just did.

It was one of those things.

A rip in time.

By the time I got up to start my walk home, the back door was crowded.

Well then. I would simply slip out the front door.

The music had started back, so everyone was busy checking their dance cards.

They certainly weren't noticing me—the man who was known for having little interest in society.

I got as far as the foyer when the clock began to chime again.

It wasn't possible that an hour could have passed already.

Not possible at all.

I stopped and looked past the clock, up the stairway.

The clouds shifted just at that moment, allowing the moonlight to stream in through the window.

It was her.

Sophia stood on the landing... wearing the beautiful silver ballgown again.

I grinned.

I could not help myself.

My world had just shifted back into place.

42

SOPHIA

I had no explanation for why I wanted to wander the halls.

I think it was the garden that lured me outside. The garden and the memory of what had happened with Nathan. I couldn't stop thinking about Nathan and that kiss.

As I walked down the hallway toward the stairs, feeling rather proud of the way I deftly maneuvered my hoop skirts. In the event that I did ever go back in time, I would most certainly be much more prepared than I had been last time.

As I reached the stairs, light orchestra music drifted up.

Was Grandpa up late after all? Playing music in his study perhaps?

I shook my head.

He'd gone into his bedroom. We'd walked upstairs together after dinner.

I placed one hand on the rail.

The sound of the music slowly increased and with it came voices and laughter.

"No." It wasn't possible.

It would be just too weird. Too improbable.

Carefully making my way down the first flight of stairs, I stopped on the landing.

The grandfather clock began chiming the hour.

The broken grandfather clock… Grandpa had been talking just tonight about calling out a different clock person to see if they could procure the illusive part from a different company. It wouldn't just spontaneously start working.

The clouds shifted, bathing me in moonlight.

Moonlight sparkled off the silvery silk of the dress as I turned, my hands at my sides, my breath coming in shallow gasps.

And right there at the bottom of the stairs stood none other than Nathan.

It was as though he'd been waiting for me.

As though he had expected me to be here, coming down the stairs at this particular moment in time.

It was not possible, of course. Not with hundreds of years separating us.

But some things could not be explained.

I couldn't move. My feet were frozen to the floor.

Nathan reached the stairs in two long strides and before I had time to catch my breath, he was standing on the landing next to me.

"How did you—"

Taking my hand, he pulled me back up the stairs and down the hallway.

"Where are we going?" I asked, realizing I was smiling.

His hand was firm on mine. I wasn't sure I could have pulled away if I'd wanted to. But I didn't want to.

We reached the door to my bedroom, but he didn't open it.

Instead, he pulled me close, just as he had done in the gardens, a palm splayed across my cheek.

"She was right," he said.

Then he gently lowered his lips to mine, our breath mingling.

He smelled like cigars and whiskey, and something unique to him. Husky. His soap, perhaps.

"How do I keep you here?" he asked.

"I don't know." My breath was shallow and I could barely catch it.

Being in his arms like this was almost more than I could bear.

"You're mine," he said.

I nodded.

Then he crushed his lips to mine.

43

NATHAN

A rooster crowed, heralding the dawn. Dogs barked as a rider came toward the house. For what purpose I didn't know, nor did I care.

I had everything I wanted right here.

Propping on my elbow, I rested my head against my fist and watched Sophia sleep.

Her soft kissable lips, were gently parted as she slept. I wrapped a finger around a strand of her long hair.

We had kissed for hours, until we'd ended up here, in her bed, exhausted.

I'd gotten her out of her dress, leaving her wearing nothing other than her chemise and had taken off my own frock coat. We'd gotten a second wind without the weight of all that clothing.

I would marry her, of course, even though we had only kissed.

I was rather pleased at my own restraint, but I knew that the only thing keeping me from ravishing her had been my love for her.

It was an odd phenomenon that I had never experienced before.

We would have plenty of time for lovemaking after I made her my wife.

It was important to me that she be respected.

I would send for a priest so that we wouldn't have to wait. I didn't want to wait.

As I watched her stir in her sleep, I contemplated how I might make sure that she stayed here… in this time.

I couldn't hold her hand every moment.

I had nothing.

The only thing that I could use to bind her to me was our love.

Vaughn seemed to think that had something to do with it, even though she confessed that she had a love in two different worlds.

Did Sophia have someone in her own time? If she did, then this was going to be more difficult than it seemed.

Unable to keep my hands off her, I leaned forward and placed a light kiss on her brow.

But it was enough to wake her.

She opened her eyes and smiled at me.

Mon Dieu.

The way she looked at me with those eyes.

"Good morning," she said.

"Good morning, my love," I said.

She smiled then. So soft and sweet.

I lost myself in those green eyes of hers.

I wanted to fall in and never leave.

"What do we do now?" she asked.

I brushed a thumb over her swollen lips.

"I can think of a few things," I said.

"Not that." But she didn't pull away.

I leaned in and kissed her.

And by the time we came up for air, a ray of sunshine glimmered through the window.

"First of all," I said. "We have to make this official."

"How do we do that?" she asked.

I rolled off the bed and got down on one knee.

"Marry me," I said.

44

SOPHIA

It was barely daylight and it was so quiet.

No distant roar of the air conditioner. No television noises. Just quiet.

It still had that feeling of a power outage to me. The air was raw and humid.

The window was up a few inches, letting in some fresh air along with the scent of flowers in the garden.

It was interesting to me that Grandpa planted flowers similar to what the Becquerels had planted hundreds of years ago.

The more things changed, the more they stayed the same.

This world seemed surreal.

But not Nathan.

Nathan was real and virile. Strong. Protective.

As I searched Nathan's cobalt blue eyes, my breath hitched.

He took my hands in his and looked up at me.

Despite the fact that I was wearing nothing more than a lightweight chemise, having him kneel on one knee to propose was wordlessly romantic.

I was so overcome, in fact, that I could not answer.

"I don't want to wait," he said, kissing the backs of my fingers.

I shook my head and a veil of peacefulness draped over me.

"I don't want to wait either."

I had to believe that there was a reason why I had not only come back in time, but I had met Nathan.

We'd had a sudden, irrefutable attraction. Something that didn't normally happen. At least not to me.

Maybe I was crazy. Maybe I wouldn't be able to stay in the past with him for more than a short time.

But either way, nothing said I could not enjoy it while it lasted.

Life was made to be enjoyed, after all, and I'd never been one to be afraid to do what I wanted to do.

I'd wanted to be an architect in what was primarily a man's world and I'd done it without a hitch.

The first time I'd gone back in time, I'd had nothing to do with it. An accident, perhaps. But this time I had chosen it.

I had put on the ballgown and sought it out.

I had decided.

And somehow it had worked.

"So?" Nathan asked, his eyes full of love. "Will you? Will you be my wife?"

"Yes," I leaned forward, falling into his arms.

I sat on his knee, and he dipped me backwards, pressing his lips on one corner of my mouth. That little kiss sent uncontrollable tremors through me.

I couldn't get enough of him.

And if we were to be married, we could be together every day. Every day and every night. The realization left me feeling slightly giddy.

He was looking at me again… in that way that made me feel like I was truly the only woman in the world.

Then I remembered something.

"What did you mean when you said she was right?"

His expression held surprise, like he'd forgotten all about it.

"Vaughn," he said.

I sat up. "Wait. Vaughn?"

"Yes." He scooped me up and carried me over to the armchair so that I was sitting in his lap.

"Vaughn Becquerel?"

"The one and only."

"But… how?"

Vaughn was supposed to have passed away.

"I think she's out there, traveling through time," he said. "going to different places."

The statement sent goosebumps along my skin. The thought of my grandmother floating about through time was unfathomable.

And I wasn't sure how I felt about it.

"Wow," I said, putting a hand over my eyes. "I don't…"

"She's the one who told me to go to the ball. That you would be there."

I would have to think about that. Another reason to think it was more than just chance that I had come back in time and met Nathan.

"I hadn't met her before…so… I don't know if this helps or not, but Vaughn looked really good. Beautiful. Content even."

I nodded and looked into his eyes.

"That does help. Thank you. So… that's why you were there?"

He shifted me in his lap. Kissed my forehead.

"It was absolutely why. I've been keeping busy. And I had no interest in socializing."

I bit my lip and studied him. A handsome man like him would no doubt have lots of ladies trying to snare him into marriage.

"Then I guess I'm a lucky girl," I said.

He pressed his forehead against mine.

"Actually I'm the lucky one."

45

NATHAN

By mid-morning, I'd changed my mind.

It made me a nervous wreck, but I left Sophia to return to my own house. She had to get dressed as did I.

Instead of sending for the priest to come to us, I'd decided that we would go to him.

If we were going to get married today, we were going to break all sorts of rules and the less my family knew about it, the less explaining and justifying I would have to do.

I walked home, my boots crunching on the dried leaves. Everything looked so beautiful. The flowers in the garden. The silver moss hanging from the oak trees.

I was in love and the world looked so much different through that lens than it had the past few months while I'd waited for Sophia to return.

Biscuit dashed up, licked my fingers, then took off running after a squirrel.

I stopped at the well for a pail of water before going inside my house.

Sophia would like this house. I hadn't done any decorating

at all. It would be all hers to do. A lady liked to do her own decorating.

As I heated water I gathered up a clean shirt and socks. Since I'd worn my best pants and frock coat last night, I would just wear them again.

Then I went back to watch the water boil so I could shave and wash up.

I was counting on Sophia still being there when I got back. If she wasn't, what was the point really?

What would be the point of first finding her and second falling in love with her? And then finding her again?

There had to be more to it than that.

A man had to have faith in some things.

So in spite of my instinct to keep her attached to me, I'd left her alone to give her time to get herself ready for the trip into town.

The water finally hot enough, I poured some into a basin and carefully shaved my face. Wouldn't do to have nicks on my skin on my wedding day.

For a man who had avoided socializing for so long, I had absolutely no reservations about marrying Sophia.

It was just one of those things that felt right. More right than anything I had ever done.

Before I became a recluse, I'd been described as being decisive.

I had moved up here, made a deal with my uncle for some land, and not only built my own house, but I'd started my own mill. Nobody in the south started their own mill. They just sent their crops up north and let the northerners take it from there.

Then they bought back cloth made from their own cotton. Or indigo. Or whatever their crop was.

So it didn't surprise me that I was decisive about Sophia. She was simply the one I'd been waiting for.

I put on a clean white shirt and took my time buttoning it.

I didn't have a ring. My older brother had my grandmother's ring. Keeping it for whoever he decided to marry. If he even did. He wasn't showing any inclination in that direction.

I hadn't either. Our mother probably wondered where she had gone wrong.

Fortunately, there was still time for both of us to be married.

I might pen a letter to them. Let them know I was married.

Had to get the deed done first, though.

I pulled on my shoes. Tied them.

I'd taken my time to give Sophia some time, but I grew impatient to get back to her.

Being with her. Kissing her. Those things made me want her even more.

Ready, headed out the door.

It was quiet outside. And dark clouds had gathered in the west.

I whistled for Biscuit, but the dog didn't join me on my walk back to the main house.

46

SOPHIA

I sat at the vanity and slowly brushed my hair.

Today was my wedding day. Certainly not what I would have expected.

And even though I hadn't been one of those little girls who planned her wedding before puberty, there were certain things that I had just sort of taken for granted during those rare occasions when I had actually thought about it.

I wasn't completely opposed to the idea, after all.

The first thing, of course, was family. My two sisters should be here. Even my annoying older brother. My parents and their new spouses.

And flowers. Lots and lots of white flowers.

A dress, of course. A white mermaid dress.

Okay. Maybe I had thought about it a little bit.

But the husband was the most important piece and since I had that, nothing else really mattered for what would amount to five minutes of vows.

And since I only had the one dress—a lovely silver—I got back into it.

Definitely not what I was used to. I had always been a wear it one time and put it in the wash kind of girl.

But when in the 1800s…

Hearing a dog barking outside, I went to the open window and looked out.

The same dog I'd seen before sat at the edge of the woods looking at me. A shiver shot up my spine.

It was an odd thing, having that dog sitting there looking at me like that.

Then there were the clouds rolling in from the west.

I'd been caught in these storms far too much lately.

Maybe going into town wasn't such a good idea right now. Even if it was to get married.

I'd heard someone say that getting married in the rain was good luck.

Whoever had said that hadn't had to ride a horse or ride in a buggy to get there.

The clock chimed through the house. It was ten o'clock.

A horse and rider came from the stables around back and galloped down the road toward the river.

Nathan should have been back by now. He'd promised he'd only be gone a short time.

Turning, I looked around the room. I was definitely still in the past. No light fixtures. No electrical outlets. No bathroom or closets.

I turned back toward the window.

The dog was gone.

Then I saw Nathan walking back toward the house.

If we were going to go, at least maybe we could get ahead of the rain.

I dashed out the door, down the hallway, and slowed as I made my way down the stairs.

Eager to see Nathan again, even though he'd barely been

gone much more than an hour, I reached the first floor and hurried through the foyer and turned toward the back door.

Aunt Eloise came out of the parlor, just as I started toward the door.

"Hello," she said, with obvious surprise.

"Hi. Aunt Eloise," I said with a smile. "It's good to see you again."

"My apologies," Aunt Eloise said. "but I don't know you."

My smile faltered.

"Oh," I said. How could she possibly not remember me?

Nathan had told her we were to be married.

And if that hadn't made an impression, surely me vanishing in front of her would.

"I'm Sophia. Nathan's fiancé." Saying the words out loud felt odd. Almost as though I was pretending.

Imposter syndrome. I hadn't felt that since my first architect student practicum.

It had quickly faded, though, as I got caught up in the project I was working on with a team of other students.

But what was I supposed to do about not being recognized by the one person other than Nathan that I had actually met in this time?

Aunt Eloise looked at me blankly for a moment, then laughed.

"My dear," she said. "Nathan is one of the least marriage inclined men I know. If he were engaged, I would certainly know it."

Of course she would. And that did nothing to help matters.

A tall lanky man dressed in a black suit came around the corner and stopped.

"Missus Eloise," he said. "This is Sophia Becquerel. She's come here to visit us from Boston."

"Of course," Aunt Eloise said. "Well, if you think Nathan is inclined toward marriage, you might want to think again."

I looked at Villars with his kind face back to Aunt Eloise.

This ranked up there as one of the most bizarre conversations I'd ever had.

I had spent time talking to Aunt Eloise. She had given me this dress. Grandma Vaughn's dress, no less. She'd helped me get into it. Her and Abigail.

Surely they didn't see so many people out here that they would forget me in a matter of merely months.

"I'll show you into the parlor," Villars said. "You can wait for Mr. Nathan there."

"Okay," I said. I was getting the sense that Villars was trying to rescue me from Aunt Eloise.

I followed Villars into the parlor and sat on the sofa.

After I thanked him, he went on his way.

I sat and waited for an hour. Until the clock began to chime again.

Eleven chimes.

But Nathan did not return.

And the sliver of doubt that Aunt Eloise had planted in my brain wound its way in deep and took hold.

47

NATHAN

I stood on the back veranda. The black storm clouds gathering overhead.

My uncle had stopped me before I entered the house.

"What is it?"

Uncle Samuel thrust a letter at me.

"This just came. Your family is on the way here."

I made a quick calculation. My family only visited in Summer, arriving in spring. But this was fall.

My family had no reason to be here now.

"What do you mean?" I tried to clear my head. "Why?"

"Read the letter," he said.

I took the letter and, straightening it, leaned against the railing.

I didn't have time for this.

Whatever it was, surely it could wait.

But why would my family be coming to visit in the fall?

The immediate recognition of my father's handwriting brought me back to earth.

I read the letter. Then read it a second time.

It was only three short paragraphs—leaving a lot of things open.

"They'll be here today," Uncle Samuel said.

I turned the letter over. There was nothing on the back.

"Why do you think that? There's no date on this letter."

Uncle Samuel waved a hand in dismissal.

"The messenger who brought it."

I shook my head. "The rider who just left here?"

I'd seen the horse and rider, but paid them little heed. Messengers came and went all the time.

Uncle Samuel nodded. "That's right. They will be here today."

I looked at the letter again.

"What do you think this means?"

"I don't really know. But I do know that my sister would not have agreed to this without a good reason."

His sister. My mother. He was so right.

My mother liked routine. Liked order.

The fact that not only she and Father, but also my two brothers and my sister were on their way up here…today… was odd, to say the least.

"True," I murmured, pressing my fingers against my brow.

It was rather hard to think about my family when the woman I was going to marry was waiting upstairs for me.

And not only was she waiting, the longer we were apart, the greater the chance that she could vanish again… back to her own time.

"I have to go," I said.

Uncle Samuel dropped into the rocker behind him. Took a cigar out of his pocket and sniffed it.

His movements seemed so slow. Almost deliberately so, even though I knew he wasn't being deliberate.

He merely didn't understand my sense of urgency.

"You might as well have a seat," he said. "They're going to be here shortly. And I'm certain they will offer an explanation."

One hand on my hip, the other on the railing, I looked at my uncle.

He had no idea the predicament he was putting me in.

And just when I was about to excuse myself and go inside, I heard the mournful sound of a steamboat whistle coming from down the river.

"There," Uncle Samuel said. "They'll be here momentarily. And we can find out what is going on with them."

"Yes," I said. "we can."

My uncle did not understand. I had things I needed to be doing.

48

SOPHIA

Standing at the French window, overlooking the front of the house, I watched the storm clouds move overhead, sending the silver moss dancing in the wind.

It was odd really, how the moss tended to be attracted to the older trees more than the younger ones. They twisted around the limbs and became part of the tree.

The mournful sound of a steamboat drifted up the river, reminding me of *when* I was.

I was in the past. I didn't know how I'd gotten here and I didn't know if I could ever get home again.

And I wasn't even sure if I wanted to get home again.

I paced to the piano. Ran a finger along the ivory keys.

Maybe I should have bothered to take lessons like my younger sister. A little late to worry about that now.

Where was Nathan?

I'd been worrying about me vanishing to another time, but he was the one who wasn't here when he was supposed to be.

If he was gone, what purpose did I have in being here?

I only wanted to be here because of him.

Without him, I didn't have any reason to be in the past.

The clock began to chime the hour again.

Another hour had passed.

And I was still alone.

I had no place to go. Without him, I would be stranded here.

With him, I would be content here.

It was such an odd predicament.

I should want to find my way home, to my own time, but instead, I found myself staring out the window.

Waiting.

Waiting for Nathan.

"Can I get you anything, Miss?" Villars asked, coming to the door.

"No," I said. "Do you know when Nathan might be back?"

Villars straightened. "I'll let him know you're waiting," he said, then backed out of the room.

The door was open, yet I felt like a prisoner.

Aunt Eloise didn't recognize me, so I was a stranger to her. This was her home.

I would need her blessing to stay here.

I pressed a palm against my forehead.

Staying here would require her permission.

But I was getting ahead of myself.

Villars seemed to know where Nathan was.

I took a deep steading breath and went sit on the sofa.

Nathan no doubt had things to do.

It wasn't his fault that I wasn't used to waiting without anything to do. A phone to entertain me… Text messages to check… Music to play…

49

NATHAN

The steamboat was getting closer and it was slowing as it neared my uncle's dock.

Uncle Samuel was up, standing with one hand against a tall white column, waiting for the two horses he had sent for to take us to the dock to meet my family.

"Mr. Nathan," Villars, the butler said, coming to stand next to me. "Miss Sophia is waiting for you in the parlor."

A boy brought the two horses around and stood waiting with them.

"Let's go," Uncle Samuel said, suddenly gaining speed as he headed toward the horses. He glanced up at the dark clouds heading this way.

The wind whipped fallen leaves across the lawn, bringing an unapologetic energy with it.

"If we go now," he said. "we can have them back before the bottom falls out."

The rain. He was right. Getting caught in the storm was unavoidable, no matter how quickly we left.

"I can't," I said. "I'll have to catch up with you."

Dire circumstances.

That's what the letter said.

I was torn between loyalty to my family and my devotion to Sophia.

Sophia was waiting for me. Already, I'd made her wait longer than I'd planned.

My family needed me.

Something unforeseen had happened. Something that sent them north. My family had never come north other than during the summer.

I had obligations.

But even my obligations weren't going to keep me from Sophia.

"Suit yourself," Uncle Samuel said, looping the reins of one horse around the hitching post before mounting the other one.

Having made my decision, I hurried in through the back door and headed straight to the parlor.

The grandfather clock began to chime the hour just as I crossed through the foyer.

Sophia stood up as I reached the door.

She wore the lovely silver dress again and my heart caught in my throat at the sight of her.

Relief flooded through me that she was still here as I closed the distance between us.

As I pulled her into my arms, her dress flowed backwards with yards and yards of silk.

Her arms wrapped around my waist and she laid her head against my chest.

She sighed.

"I apologize," I said. "There was a letter from my family."

"Is something wrong?" she asked, leaning back to search my eyes.

"I don't know," I said. "They're here. Arriving on the steamboat as we speak."

"You need to go," she said, pressing her cheek against my chest again.

She held me like she would never let me go.

"Yes," I said, holding her back.

We didn't have to say it, but both of us knew that between the storm and my family's unexpected arrival, the wedding would have to wait.

Even though I didn't want to let her go, I couldn't ask her to go out into the storm with me.

And I couldn't not go.

50

SOPHIA

Standing on the back veranda, beneath the shelter of the balcony above, I watched Nathan go into the storm and mount the dapple-gray horse that stood waiting.

Sitting on the back of the horse, he looked across at me, his eyes holding promises.

I fought the urge to run into the rain and wind just to touch his hands one more time before he rode off.

He would be back. I knew that.

Yet I could not deny the feelings of loss that settled into the pit of my stomach.

I didn't want to be apart from him.

I shook my head. It was irrational.

As he turned I held up a hand and forced a smile on my face.

When he returned the smile, some of the weight lightened off my heart.

A gust of wind whipped at my skirts and tossed my hair into my eyes. It brought the first heavy drops of rain with it.

Not wanting to get drenched from the blowing wind, I went back inside.

I'd go to my bedroom—the guest room—and wait.

No need to distress Aunt Eloise by my presence.

Villars met me at the foot of the stairs.

"Miss Sophia," he said. "There's someone waiting to see you in the parlor."

He kept his expression blank, a skill that I envied.

"For me?" Who could be here to see me?

"She specifically asked me to bring you to see her."

"Who is it?" I asked, following Villars.

"I'm not sure if you know her or not," Villars said, stepping aside for me to go into the parlor before him.

A woman stood next to the fireplace. She wore a long dress, much like mine, but she also wore a long cloak with a hood over her head.

I reached out and grabbed the door frame to steady myself.

This woman looked familiar.

"Grandma?"

She swept the hood off her head, letting it fall back.

I gasped.

It was my grandmother Vaughn and she held out her arms.

I went to her, my heart pounding so fast I could hear my own blood in my ears.

I stopped a foot away from her and looked at her. Just looked at her.

She looked… good. Younger.

"How?"

She smiled.

"Time travel can be a wonderful thing."

Time travel.

She was alive right now. In this moment.

Absolutely astounded, I walked into her hug.

51

NATHAN

Traveling in the rain had to be up there in the list of most miserable things a person had to endure.

I liked a good rain storm as much as the next man as long as I didn't have to get out in it. Which was pretty much rarely.

There always seemed to be some kind of obligation calling me out anytime it rained.

Today was no different.

Coming from the dock, my house was closer than the main Becquerel house, so we stopped there while Uncle Samuel stayed behind to take care of some business.

Using dry kindling, I started a fire in the fireplace to chase off some of the dampness.

I got my mother and sister settled into my guest room while my brothers and Father used my bedroom to dry off and put on dry clothes.

They each carried a valise, but they didn't appear to have brought trunks with them. That was just another peculiarity about their trip.

I wanted Sophia here with me. Couldn't wait, in fact, for her to meet my family.

But again… the storm.

So I used the time to straighten up. Straightened and stacked some newspaper on the table. Put water on to boil for tea.

I still didn't know what had brought my family here, but in good time, they would tell me. They looked tired, though that came as no surprise.

The trip up on a steamboat was a feat to be endured… certainly not for the faint of heart.

I added another log to the fireplace, dusted my hands off and checked the boiling water.

If they were only staying a short time, they could stay here, but otherwise, the house wasn't guest ready. I still had empty bedrooms, yet to be furnished with even the basics like beds.

Besides, I couldn't see any reason why they would have made this trip for only a short time. Any news could surely be shared by letters.

My younger sister, Isabella, was the first one to come out to the parlor. She had changed into a dark gray day dress with a high neckline. Very genteel.

At seventeen, she was the belle of every ball down in New Orleans. She hated it up here in what she called *the north.*

"Nice place," she said, taking a seat on the sofa.

Isabella seemed to grow up a little bit more every time I saw her.

"Thank you," I said. "Can I get you some tea?"

"Do you have anything stronger?" she asked. "Some bourbon perhaps?"

I had to give myself credit for keeping my jaw from dropping.

Normally, I would have thought she was jesting, but first of all, my sister was not the jesting sort. She was actually very serious, a trait that men seemed unable to resist.

And second, I knew when a person was jesting, and Isabella was not jesting.

"Of course," I said. "In your tea? Surely you don't want Mother or Father to know."

She shrugged. "Sure. You can put it in the tea."

I made my little sister a cup of tea and added a shot of bourbon. Handed it to her just as our Father joined us.

He was followed by my older brother Grant and my younger brother, Andrew. A minute later, our mother joined us.

"I'll get it," Mother said when I offered to pour hot tea for them. "We have something to tell you."

I sat down next to my sister.

Father, his hands behind his back, paced to the fireplace and back. Mother brought a tray of teacups and set it carefully on the coffee table.

"We're going to be moving up here," Father said.

I looked from him to my mother and back. They all looked incredibly serious.

And I was reminded that they would not have come all this way merely to joke with me.

"Why?" I asked. "What's happened?"

"The plantation house burned," Grant said, in his matter-of-fact way.

"What? When?"

"Three weeks ago," Father said.

"Why didn't someone send for me?" I asked.

"It all happened so fast," Mother said, handing me a mug of hot tea. "And we didn't know what we were going to do."

I looked down at the tea and was suddenly quite envious of my sister's shot of bourbon.

"What are you going to do?"

"We sold the townhouse," Grant said.

I looked at my father, but he was deferring to my older brother.

"I don't understand."

"There's nothing left for us there," Grant said. "Not without the house."

"You could rebuild," I said.

Grant glanced at Father.

"We had some debts to pay."

"So… there's not enough money to rebuild?"

"Not the way we wanted to," Grant said, taking a sip of his coffee, then shrugged. "Thought you could probably use some help."

"Just tell him," Mother said looking at Father as she sat next to him and they linked hands.

"When we were married," Father said. "Your mother's dowry was a section of land."

For the second time this morning, my jaw nearly dropped to the floor.

"Did you know about this?" I asked Grant.

Grant shook his head.

I looked at my parents.

"Why didn't you tell us about this?" I asked.

Mother glanced around, looking at each of us in turn.

"I loved your father," she said.

No one said a word. It was quiet enough to hear a pin drop. She wasn't telling us anything we didn't know.

"And I was afraid something would happen to separate us."

My stomach clenched with dread at what she was going to say.

And I had a feeling I knew what she was going to say even before she said it.

"I carry the Becquerel blood."

52

SOPHIA

I sat on the sofa next to my grandmother, our hands linked.

I still could not wrap my head around her actually here. Alive.

But that was the power of time travel. If I could believe in time travel, I could believe that my grandmother was here now.

"How are you here?" I asked.

"It's not the how so much as the why," she said. "The how is complicated."

"Why then?"

"I have to tell you something."

My heart shuddered.

"What is it?" I asked, although I really wasn't sure I wanted to know.

"You need to get back to the future. For Grandpa Jonathan."

"Is he in trouble? Is his life in danger?" I clutched her hands. I had no control over this. No control over this time travel that had brought me here.

A spell they had said.

"No. But I don't want you to have regrets."

I shook my head, my eyes welling with unshed tears.

"You need to say goodbye to him."

I'd never felt such helplessness.

"How?" I breathed.

"I'll show you," she said with a little smile.

"Why can't you help him?" I asked.

"It's not for me to choose," she said.

"What can I do?"

Vaughn glanced out the window. The storm still brewed, thunder rumbling in the distance.

"We have a few minutes," she said. "Are you happy here?" She searching my eyes. "With Nathan?"

I didn't even ask how she knew about knew about Nathan.

Apparently she could not only do anything, she knew everything.

"Yes," I said.

"You love him?"

I felt the flush creep over my cheeks.

"Yes," I said.

"Good," she said, patting my hand.

"But Grandma?" I took a deep breath. "How can I do both?"

She smiled a slow, but sad smile.

"That's something only you can determine."

"But—"

"It's time," she said, releasing my hands and reaching into her pocket.

"Time for what?"

She held out her palm. She held a simple bronze key with a loop on one end and two connected prongs on the other end.

"This is the key," she said, taking the key and pressing it in my hand.

"The key?" The key was heavy in my hand, but warm. Warm from Vaughn's touch.

"Yes," Vaughn said, glancing toward the window again as lightning flashed through the glass.

"Grandma?" I said. "Tell me what to do."

"The clock," she said. "Put the key in the clock. Then in the second between the lightning flash and following thunder, turn the clock back one hour."

"But—"

Vaughn stood up. Put her hands on my shoulders. "This has taken a long time to sort out. But you have to trust me."

"But what lightning? What thunder?"

"When lightning flashes into the foyer… like it just did in here, turn the hands back one hour."

"What will happen?"

"I'm sorry, Sophia." She took her hands off my shoulders and took two steps back. "I don't have time to explain any further. Just do it."

She started to fade.

Literally.

"Grandpa needs you."

Then she was gone.

I sat there a moment, staring blankly into space. The space where Grandma had just stood.

Thunder rumbled outside.

Grandpa needed me.

I looked down at the key glimmering in my hand.

Without further hesitation, I got up and, maneuvering my long, full skirts, went into the foyer.

I stood looking up at the grandfather clock, the pendulum steady swinging.

Grandpa was in trouble.

The thought kept resonating in my head.

I looked over my shoulder, but there was no one there.

I opened the glass door protecting the face of the clock.

I found the keyhole at the corner of the clock's face and slid the key into it.

One thing down.

Lightning flashed through the window.

My heart pounding dangerously in my chest, I raised my arm and put a fingertip on the clock's hand.

Taking a deep breath, I twirled it back one hour.

Thunder crashed.

Looking to the right, I saw Villars standing there. Staring at me. His expression blank.

Then he faded and vanished.

Actually… I faded and vanished.

53

NATHAN

Two hours later, the storm had passed and we sat quietly in armchairs and the sofa in my living room.

Needing some air, I went out back and stood on my veranda overlooking the Mississippi River.

Two long hours of talking about time travel had left us all exhausted and overwhelmed.

My siblings had voiced a lot of disbelief, but my mother had told them the story of Vaughn and how her life had been saved by a spell that made a rip in time.

Not ready to reveal what I knew about Sophia, I'd kept my mouth shut. I'd actually learned a few things.

They hadn't come right out and said it, but I put everything together and learned that the spell had a way of bringing soul mates together.

I found that interesting on a personal note.

But my mother insisted that she had not traveled through time to meet my father.

In fact, the only question I asked during that two hours was whether or not Mother traveled through time.

Nonetheless. my mother and father had moved to New Orleans to prevent it happening to her.

They hadn't wanted to risk it.

Eventually after they had four children, they started visiting my uncle again. My mother seemed to be out of danger of traveling through time.

They actually came to believe that the spell had faded.

Little did they know.

But now they had little choice but to return to her roots… and their section of land.

Father came outside to join me. Took out two cigars and handed one to me.

I sniffed it, but didn't light it.

"Why didn't someone bother to tell me that Father owned land adjacent to Uncle Samuel?"

Father smiled.

"How do you think you were able to work a deal with Uncle Samuel?"

I turned to stare at my father.

"Are you telling me that this is actually your land?"

"Don't blame your uncle," Father said. "You mother swore him to secrecy when she asked him to help you."

Turning, I blew out a breath.

"I'm not blaming anyone," I said. "I just feel like someone should have told me."

Father scoffed as he lit his cigar.

"Not exactly the kind of thing parents want to tell their children."

"Would make a good bedtime story," I said.

Father just looked at me.

"I guess if one wanted their children to grow up with fanciful notions."

"Not fanciful if it's true," I muttered.

One thing I knew for certain. I might not tell my children

straight out about the time travel that ran through the Becquerel blood, but…

I froze.

It occurred to me that if my mother carried Becquerel blood.

So did I.

54

SOPHIA

I stood in front of the grandfather clock, staring blankly at the rip between the six and seven. A rip that hadn't been there an instant earlier.

The clock had been damaged in the Civil War and as a tribute to the travesty of the losses during that time, it had never been repaired.

I was home. I was back to my time.

Grandpa.

I whirled around and called out his name.

Sunlight coming in through the window blinded me as the cool air blew over me from the air conditioning vent over my head.

"Grandpa!" I called his name again. I looked up the stairs, but wearing this dress, it would be easier for me to look for him downstairs first.

I looked in the parlor first. He wasn't there.

The television seemed so odd and out of place in the old house.

It had taken me no time at all to get used to the house the way it was back in the past.

I whirled around and went the other way, toward the back of the house.

I looked into his study, into the kitchen, the library. But he wasn't in any of those rooms.

My heart was pounding. Grandma Vaughn had said he was in trouble and I didn't doubt her word. I had no reason to. She had been right about how to get back to my time.

As I reached the back door, I saw Grandpa's old green Chevrolet truck that he used around the property sitting out back.

Shoving the door open, I stepped out onto the veranda.

There he was sitting in a rocker.

"Grandpa." I ran toward him.

He blinked at me, taking in my dress.

I'd gotten used to it and had all but forgotten that I was wearing the wrong kind of clothes for this time period.

"Sophia?" he asked.

"Yes."

"You came back."

"Of course."

He looked different. Tired.

"Are you okay?" I asked, kneeling in front of him.

"Of course," he said. "It's just been so very long since I've seen you. That dress… you remind me so much of Vaughn."

"Vaughn." I wanted to tell him that I just saw her. That she looked lovely and well, but something held me back.

It was something in his eyes.

"I wasn't gone so long," I said. "What's wrong? What's happened?"

He looked at me quizzically.

"Sophia," he said. "You don't know."

I shook my head.

I didn't know what he was talking about.

"Know what?"

A flock of birds dropped to the ground into what used to be his garden.

What had happened to his garden? I didn't have time to worry about that right now.

"Sophia," he said. "You've been gone for ten years."

55

NATHAN

I hurried up the steps to the back veranda of the main house.

This thing with my family would sort itself out.

Now that it had stopped raining, they were preparing to come here where they would live until they could build a house.

I'd excused myself and came back ahead of them.

Sophia waited for me and I couldn't bear to make her wait for me any longer.

It was too late for us to go into town to be married as we'd planned and we needed to reconsider now that my family was here.

I could hardly elope with them right here. I'd leave that up to her, though, of course.

I still felt the urgency to tie her to me.

My parents were convinced that the time spell had faded and I hadn't told them anything different.

If the time travel had anything to do with finding true love, my parents were safe. I'd go to the bank on that one.

I went straight to the foyer, but there was no one there.

As I turned, the grandfather clock began to chime the hour.

The sound that was normally just background noise sent a chill through me.

I went to the clock and looked up into its face.

As the chimes faded into a distant echo, Villars came up beside me.

"Mister Nathan," he said. He looked alarmed and that was saying something for a man who had keep a blank expression down to an art.

"What is it, Villars?" I asked. Something was wrong. "Have you seen Sophia?"

"Yes, sir," he said.

He held out his hand for me. "Here."

He dropped a key into my palm.

"What's this?" I asked.

Villars nodded toward the clock.

"I found it there," he said. "in the corner of the face of the clock."

"Okay," I said. "What's it do?"

"It sets the time, Sir."

I shifted from one foot to the other. I didn't have time for this.

"I need to find Sophia," I said.

"Sir." Villars swallowed. "The key."

"What about the key?" I asked. I held it out to him, but he took a step back. Shook his head.

"Why are you giving it to me?"

"Sir. Miss Sophia had this key. She used it."

"For what?"

"To set the time, Sir."

"And?"

Villars glanced at the clock's face.

"The time's wrong now."

"What?" I tugged my pocket watch and opened the cover.

Four o'clock.

The grandfather clock showed three o'clock.

I looked back to Villars.

"Why is it wrong?"

Villars glanced over his shoulder, then leaned in closer and lowered his voice.

"She did it."

"What do you mean? Why would she change the time?"

"Sir," Villars said, not answering my question. "This key has been missing for neigh unto six years."

"Missing?"

"Yes sir." Villars straightened proudly. "But the old clock, she keeps good time, so it was of no concern."

"Villars. Who had the key?"

"I'm afraid I don't know. But it was missing."

"And Sophia had it?"

"Yes, sir. She did."

"Villars." I didn't try to hide the alarm in my voice. "Where is Sophia?"

"Gone. Vanished."

56

SOPHIA

I sat at the kitchen table, warming my hands on a hot coffee mug. The coffee smelled wonderful. A good cup of coffee was one thing I had missed in the past.

Grandpa had packed my clothes away in a corner of the closet and, of course, even after ten years, they still fit. I was wearing a pair of sweat pants and my Ralph Lauren teddy bear t-shirt.

I was up early after a sleepless night. I'd lain awake staring at the ceiling, trying to make sense of what had happened.

My Grandma Vaughn who had passed away several ago had gone into the past and had given me the secret to getting back to my own time.

She'd told me that Grandpa Jonathan needed me. But Grandpa seemed fine.

Except for being ten years older.

The best thing I had come up with was that something must have gone wrong.

There was no way that time travel could be an exact science.

Overall, it had worked.

I'd gone back to the place I'd left, just ten years later.

I'd thought a lot about time lines and such other abstract concepts. So much so that my head hurt from it.

And I hadn't figured a damn thing out.

I needed to talk to my family. My parents. My two sisters. My brother.

But I couldn't just call them out of the blue.

Not after being presumed dead for ten years.

Grandpa reported me missing.

He knew that I had gone back in time, but his options were limited and a grown man couldn't just go around talking about time travel like it was a normal occurrence.

Before I miraculously reappeared, I needed to figure out what I wanted to do.

Actually I already knew what I *wanted* to do.

I *wanted* to return to the past.

To Nathan.

I was fairly certain that if Grandma hadn't told me that Grandpa was in trouble, I wouldn't have followed her directions to come back here.

I finished my coffee and still Grandpa didn't come downstairs. Maybe now that he was older, he didn't get up so early.

I rinsed my mug and put it in the dishwasher then I wandered back toward the foyer.

It made perfect sense that if a storm and the turn of a key held the secrets of time travel to get me back here, it could also take me back to the past.

But... I stopped in front of the grandfather clock. It stood silent as it always had until I went into the past.

Would I need to turn the hands forward?

I'd turned them back to travel forward, so would the opposite hold true for going back?

Trying to impose logical on an illogical concept was difficult at best.

It made perfect sense to me.

And I was willing to try it.

All I had to do was to wait until the next storm.

57

NATHAN

I spent the next three days wandering back and forth between my house and the main Becquerel house.

I didn't eat. I barely slept.

Mostly I just walked and stared into space.

For the most part, I kept my fingers wrapped around the key in my pocket.

Somehow it made me feel closer to Sophia. She had done something with it, then she had vanished, leaving it here. It somehow held the answers to her time travel.

Villars had seen Sophia vanish just as I had that day. Just as my mother had.

For some reason Aunt Eloise did not remember Sophia

I couldn't explain that.

And I only knew because Villars had told me.

I hadn't spoken to anyone in my family since Villars had handed me the key.

I felt like I should know what to do with it, but I did not.

All I knew was that for some reason Sophia seemed to not only know what to do with it, but she had chosen to do whatever that was in order to leave this time.

I told myself she had to have a good reason for going back to her own time.

It did not help me feel any better.

We were planning to get married when she had decided to leave me to go back to her own time.

Biscuit licked my fingers as I turned down the path toward my house.

I was having trouble sitting still for more than a few minutes at the time. I only slept for a few minutes when I collapsed in exhaustion.

Then I would wake, my heart heavy.

I didn't really expect to find her as I walked the trails. Paced inside my home.

I haven't even shaved. When my younger brother pointed out to me that I was looking like a thug, I just ignored him and kept walking.

I knew my family talked about me, but they were wrapped in their own world. Trying to accept that not only did time travel run through the family, but they were destined to live here—in the north—now.

My sister was doing some pouting of her own and my older brother was staying to himself. Grant had always seen himself living and dying at the house on the River Road. Even when the family packed up and went into the city for the winter, he found a reason to stay behind.

Before reaching my house, I noticed a rumble of dark clouds in the distance.

My heart spun.

I'd come to associate storms with seeing Sophia. Someone had mentioned something about storms having something to do with the time travel.

My fingers wrapped around the key to the grandfather clock, I turned on my heel and went back the way I had just come. Biscuit, turned too, quietly and without judgment.

I patted him on the head.

"You're the only one who understands me," I told the dog.

Biscuit let out a single bark and wagged his tail as we walked companionably toward the main house.

I reached it within minutes and went inside.

The house was quiet as usual, despite having two families living under the same roof. The men spent most of their time outside in the stables or the field.

The ladies stayed in their respective bedrooms during the day, coming down for dinner.

The ladies actually seemed less concerned with all that was going on than the men did.

I went straight to the foyer, opened the glass door to the clock, and slid the key inside.

Then I waited.

For what, I didn't know.

But if there was a way for me to get Sophia, I was determined to find it.

58

SOPHIA

It had been the better part of a week since I'd returned to my time. I'd spent a great deal of time with Grandpa. As far as I could tell, he was perfectly good. He'd slowed down a lot, but considering that he was ten years older, that was a given.

I'd spent a little time on Grandpa's computer in his study exploring the Internet to see what I had missed. I hardly recognized any of the names.

We had a new president, but politics was just more of the same. There was an ongoing discussion about whether or not the world was flat. I couldn't decide if it was in jest or a serious discussion, so I reserved my opinion and moved on.

I read an article on what looked like a reputable website about the whole trip to the moon being a hoax. That was interesting, but not something relevant.

I checked the latest architectural trends, but didn't see anything groundbreaking.

Even the movie stars were all different.

In essence, I found myself in a world that was similar to the one I'd left. There was still Internet and such, but I hardly recognized the content.

I found myself much more interested in the past.

This morning Father picked Grandpa up to drive him into town to do errands. Since the time didn't seem right to reveal that I had returned, I stayed behind and out of sight.

Having the house to myself, I went into Grandpa's study and kneeled in front of an old leather trunk.

I knew that someone had brought it down from the attic a long time ago. Over ten years ago.

I opened the lid and let it fall to the back.

It was full of old stuff. What looked like a discolored wedding dress. Stacks of letters and journals. Photographs.

I plundered around, looking for something that interested me. Something from the early 1800s.

Tucked in the bottom, I found a thick, very heavy Bible.

I was kind of surprised I hadn't seen this before. And I probably would have if I'd shown the least bit of interest in history. I was the one who was only interested in the future. Maybe some here and now, but the future for sure.

Lifting it out carefully, I set the Bible on Grandpa's desk and quickly found the record pages in the middle.

The records were filled with a long list of Becquerels.

I recognized some of them. Eloise, for one.

But the names that really stood out for me were Erika and Bradley Becquerel. My older cousins.

Grandpa had told me they had gone back in time. And they were listed right here in black ink.

The names could belong to people with the same names, but I instinctively knew that they were my cousins. Their names were written in a different handwriting off to the side with little arrows pointing to their spouse.

Erika had apparently married Charles Becquerel and Bradley had married someone named Camille.

At first I didn't see Nathan's name. There was a man named Nathaniel, but that was someone different. Someone married to Vaughn.

I dropped into the chair behind me.

My grandmother had married Nathaniel Becquerel in the 1800s?

Surely it was a different Vaughn Becquerel.

Maybe not.

I smiled to myself. My grandmother was an interesting woman with an interesting life to say the least.

Did Grandpa know this?

Of course he did.

Grandpa would have wanted my Grandma to be taken care of. To be happy.

I stood up. Stretched. And walked to the window.

It looked late outside. But that was odd because it was still morning.

I checked the time. Only ten twenty-five.

I went to the back door and looked out toward the west.

Black clouds gathered over the trees and the wind was blowing sending dark gray moss dancing and spindly pine trees bending over at the tops.

There was a storm coming in.

A storm!

This was it. It was time.

I'd just checked the Weather Channel that morning when I got up. There had no rain in the forecast. None.

Weather was a lot like time travel. Not an exact science. Just had to go with what you had.

I didn't have time to put on the silver dress.

Damn.

I had on sweatpants and a t-shirt. Well. It would have to do.

I'd find something appropriate to wear when I got back to the past.

I started to head upstairs to find Grandpa to say goodbye, but a rumble of thunder crashed overhead.

There was no time.

I stopped in front of the clock and opened the little glass door.

Lightly touching the keyhole, I realized that I didn't have the key.

I'd left the key in the past.

59

NATHAN

As the rain pounded against the windows and the wind howled all around the house, I stepped into the foyer and went to stand in front of the grandfather clock.

I heard my sister, Isabella, talking to my cousin Marvin in the parlor. My cousin said something, then my sister laughed. A few seconds later, my sister started playing the piano. I knew it was her. She was playing her favorite song—a soulfully sad romantic tune. One that shattered a person's heart into a thousand pieces.

I took the key out of my pocket and slipped it into the keyhole in the bottom of the clock's face.

Now what?

A bolt of lightning flashed through the window, lighting the room. My sister kept playing. Her sad music fitting well with the dreariness of the storm.

I stared at the clock's face, looking for answers.

It wasn't giving me any.

Turning my head, I looked for Villars. Where was the man when a person needed him? He was always there, ready and willing to help.

But not at this particular moment.

I was on my own.

Turning my attention back to the clock, I closed the glass and splayed my palm across it.

Squeezing my eyes tightly closed, I thought about Sophia. I pictured her lovely green eyes and soft pink lips.

I missed her. So much.

The thought of spending the rest of my life without her was heartbreaking. And my sister's damn music wasn't helping matters.

I just didn't know what to do.

I took my hand off the glass and ran my fingers through my hair.

The storm raged all around me. Wind. Lightning. Thunder.

I knew the storm and the clock were somehow the answers to getting Sophia back, but didn't know the combination.

My sister's music began to fade as though I had walked outside and was listening to it from a distance.

I opened my eyes and turned around.

The room was misty, like early morning fog on the river.

Then I saw her, hazy at first, then slowly becoming clear.

It was Sophia.

She was standing less than two feet in front of me. Wearing pants again and the white painted shirt.

Her eyes were moist as her gaze locked onto mine.

I know she saw me, but I didn't think she believed it.

She looked so… sad.

Maybe she heard Isabella's music, too.

As I stretched out a hand for her, she held up a hand up as though to touch me.

She lowered her hand to mine, and our fingers connected.

What felt like a bolt of lightning ran right through me.

60

SOPHIA

I'd taken two steps back from the clock as hauntingly sad music drifted through the house along with the noises of the storm all around. I blinked against mist obscuring my vision.

The thunderstorm raged all around me, seeming to shake the very foundation of the house.

How had the weather forecast have been so wrong? How had it gone from such a beautiful day to a day fraught with such turbulent weather?

I couldn't see anything on either side of me.

Yet I could see right in front of me.

My feet froze in place as my brain tried to comprehend what was happening.

Nathan.

He was standing right here in front of me.

Yet I couldn't touch him.

At least not exactly.

As our hands touched, it felt like a bolt of lightning shot between us.

And maybe it did.

Lightning flashed all around us.

Nathan was right there, yet there seemed to be some kind of force between us. Keeping us apart.

Everything was hazy. Mist swirling around us.

Yet I could see Nathan clearly. I could *feel* him.

But I couldn't touch him.

It seemed like we were looking at each from different places.

Floating in time perhaps.

The piano music seemed far away, yet I could hear it so clearly.

It was hauntingly beautiful.

I took a step forward toward Nathan, but as I did, he seemed to move back.

Yet he hadn't moved.

Other than the electric touch of our hands, I couldn't get any closer to him.

"Sophia," he said, his voice clear and full of love and longing. "I thought I'd lost you."

"No," I whispered, my heart in my throat. "Never."

"Come back to me," he said.

I gazed into his deep blue eyes. Eyes that I'd fallen in love with.

"I don't know how," I said. "I don't have the key."

He looked perplexed.

"Sophia," he said. "Find a way."

Find a way.

The words echoed in my head.

They echoed in my head as I blinked.

The first thing I was aware of was that the music was more faint.

Then the mist swirled between us—between me and Nathan.

I reached out for him with both hands. But he was fading.

Or I was fading.

We were fading.

"No!" No. No.

I leaned forward, grasping for him. He held out his hands for me.

"Come back to me," he said again.

Then he was gone.

61

NATHAN

Along with the thunder and lightning of the storm, my sister's piano music sounded deafeningly loud.

The blood pounded in my ears.

I'd seen her. I'd seen Sophia.

I'd touched her hand.

Sort of.

I had *felt* her hand against mine.

What torture was this that time played on us?

Keeping us apart while tormenting us with a glimpse of each other, yet we could not touch.

How was it that we had been so close to each other?

Had we been in the same place in time?

My cousin came to the parlor door and looked at me.

"What's wrong with you?" he asked. "You look like you've seen a ghost."

I muttered something unfit for anyone's ears, and turned on my heel.

I went straight to the back door, walked across the veranda, and stepped out into the storm.

The wind whipped menacingly at my skin and the rain stabbed through my shirt like daggers.

I didn't care.

I just needed to get away from here. To get away from the place where Sophia was, but wasn't.

I'd seen her, but I hadn't been able to touch her. If I could have gotten my hands on her, I would have never let her go.

I reached into pocket for the key, but it wasn't there.

I froze right there in the garden with daisy petals scattered across the ground by the wind. My boots sank into the mud and rain ran down my face, blinding me.

I'd left the key inside. In the clock's keyhole.

It had done me no good to have it.

It was merely even more torture, knowing that she was out of my reach.

I fought past the despair. Fought it tooth and nail.

I would NOT give up.

She was still out there.

Somewhere.

The key and the storm combined together to bring us into the same space, even if only for a moment.

If it happened once, it could happen again.

And maybe next time it would happen for real.

She would find a way back to me.

I was certain of it.

Too much had transpired for it not to happen.

She was the love of my life. The only woman for me.

I had to keep believing.

And I would wait.

If need be I would wait for the rest of my life for Sophia Becquerel.

62

SOPHIA

The music stopped. And the storm moved on, taking the crashing thunder and flashing lightning with it.

It was still raining, but it was a soft rain, not the harsh blowing rain that came with the storm.

I stood there in front of the grandfather clock, staring into its ripped face.

The storm had somehow brought Nathan and me to the same place in time.

It had been like floating in a bubble of time. Just the two of us.

There had been piano music, perhaps he'd brought that from his time.

Our times had bumped together.

Just enough for us to *feel* each other.

I sat on the bottom step and replayed everything that had happened.

It merely strengthened my resolve to find a way back to him.

He and I were soul mates.

My grandmother had been soulmates with Grandpa.

Could a person have more than one soulmate?

That was not for me to know.

But I knew the answer for myself. The answer for me was no.

I had one soulmate.

Nathan.

Find a way.

He needed me to find a way back to him. I was heartened by seeing him. By his words.

By the strength of the feeling that I felt between us.

And we hadn't even actually touched.

Not really.

Yet an electricity had shot between us.

Had he felt it, too?

He had to.

The strength of the connection had been too strong for him not to.

If only I had the key.

I got up and went to stand in front of the clock, looked up into its face.

I opened the glass door.

Was that…?

I reached up and… yes… it was.

It was the key.

Pulling it out, I held it in my palm where it seemed to glimmer with energy.

Somehow, through the magical power of time travel, Nathan had brought me the key.

Closing my fingers, clutching the key in my hand, I took it back to the steps and sat down again.

Now all I needed was a storm.

I had the key and the storm.

The rest of it I would figure out.
No matter what it took.
I would figure it out.

63

NATHAN

Six months later

Despite my dislike for social gatherings, I felt compelled to attend all of those held by the Becquerels.

Tonight they were holding a ball, mostly for my sister, Isabella.

She was eighteen now and in need of a husband before she teetered over the edge of becoming an old maid.

They had invited all the families with eligible bachelors in both north Mississippi and north Louisiana.

Their house was quite crowded. All the families were eager to meet the belle of New Orleans and I had to say that my sister looked absolutely beautiful tonight, even if she was my sister.

She wore a blue glittering gown and matching hat. So many men gathered around her, vying for her attention. I felt sorry for them, one and all. My sister, although she was of age, had no interest in getting married.

Getting married would take her away from here.

If she was going to go anywhere, it would be back to New Orleans. She'd told me so herself on enough occasions. Not a member of my family had a single doubt about her views on marriage.

I stood off to the side, near the tall open French door so that I could slip out into the clear autumn air if need be.

And by need by I meant if any young ladies decided that I might be a candidate for a husband. I felt sorry for them, too, with all the beaus gathered around my sister, there were no men left to fill their dance cards.

I shook my head. After the dancing started, assuming my sister allowed anyone to fill a slot on her dance card, they would disperse back among the young ladies they were accustomed to.

My sister would be like that, one day, I mused, unless my sister found herself engaged.

The three-man orchestra had gathered in preparation for the first reel.

My sister excused herself and floated toward me.

"Would you be my escort for a moment, Brother?" she asked.

"Of course," I said, holding out my arm for her to tuck her hand in the crook of my elbow.

We walked across the veranda, leaving the bevy of suitors behind us.

"Where am I having the privilege of taking my enviable sister?"

"I doubt too many envy me," she said. "I think all the women wish I were dead."

"You always did have a way of cutting to the heart of things," I said as we walked down the steps to the gardens.

"I told them to leave me. That I had no interest in dancing," she said.

"That only made them want you all the more," I said.

"Is that really how it works?" she asked. "If it is, then all the women in two states should be after you."

"It would do them no good."

After removing her hand from my elbow, she leaned against the wood fence railing, her hoop skirted dress belling out behind her.

"Mother thinks you're waiting for someone," she said. "a girl."

"Mother should not tell everything she thinks," I murmured, mostly to myself. "So tell me," I said to turn the conversation back to her. "Which one of these fine young men are you going to allow to court you?"

Isabella scoffed.

"None of them. You know I have no interest."

"Surely one of them has piqued your interest."

She rolled her eyes. "About as much as one of the ladies has piqued yours."

I stood with my back against the fence, propping my elbows on the top rung.

The full moon kept the early evening darkness at bay. It would be a long night, but not so much for me.

The guests spilled out the French doors onto the back veranda along with the lively music.

My gaze wandered to the window at the stairway.

Startled, I stood up straight.

Sophia.

64

SOPHIA

Hiding out wasn't as odd as I had expected. UPS made regular stops at our door.

I'd been active my entire life, working even through college. Now I fell into a routine with my grandfather.

We would get every morning and have coffee together. Sometimes, weather permitting we'd sit outside on the veranda, but most days we sat inside at the breakfast table and watched the sun rise.

He still got a newspaper—a real printed one—so we spent an hour or so reading that together. In the process, I was caught up enough that I could have integrated back into the world if I'd wanted to.

But I didn't.

Then Grandpa would go outside and putter in his garden. I helped him at first until he got things back under control.

He talked about his life with Vaughn. About how she would come and go and he would provide cover stories for her.

After lunch, Grandpa would go upstairs to take a nap. I'd stay down in the study, sometimes napping, sometimes reading old journals and letters Grandpa had been keeping all these years. I also spent a LOT of time reading and studying.

Then after we cooked together, we'd settle into the parlor to watch a movie.

All through the day, Nathan was there in my thoughts.

But tonight was different.

Tonight I'd woken in the middle of the night to a roiling thunderstorm. My heart pounding in my ears, I jumped out of bed, and raced to the window.

It was most definitely a bad storm.

Exactly what I'd been waiting for.

I had everything I needed stored on a shelf just inside my closet.

I kept the key on a ribbon tied around my neck. Something I never wanted to lose or misplace.

I grabbed the silver dress and tugged it on over my head.

I'd packed a crossbody bag with things I considered necessary. One of them was a Kindle loaded with hundreds of eBooks with a solar panel case. It also had a first aid kit including antibiotics that Grandpa had helped me get. I was off the grid, but no one questioned an older man about needing medications for various things.

I put on the dress and laced on a pair of nice looking, rugged hiking boots that were supposed to last forever.

I tossed the bag over my arm and raced from the room. I dashed down the hallway to the stairs. Halfway down, at the landing, I stopped.

Is this what I really wanted to do?

Did I really want to leave Grandpa forever? I'd gotten really close to him over the last few months. And now I was going to leave him. Just like that.

It made me feel a little bit sick.

I put one hand on the window sill and took deep breaths to steady myself.

Lightning flashed through the glass. I jumped, but held my ground as the thunder crashed behind it.

Then everything went quiet. Even the noise of the storm.

Feeling off balance, I gripped the window frame.

Then it was noisy again. But not noise from the storm.

There was music. And conversation. And laughter.

I was outside, through the moonlight to the gardens below.

There were people outside.

A woman in an elegant long gown was first to catch my attention. Then I saw a man standing next to her.

Not just any man.

Nathan.

And he was looking up at me.

I'd gone back in time. And I hadn't even needed the key around my neck.

But I was too late.

He'd already found another.

65

NATHAN

Even though it only took about two seconds for me to dash inside, past the people milling about, some dancing, some not, it felt like an eternity.

By the time I reached the bottom of the stairs, Sophia was gone.

I turned and looked over my shoulder, but I if she'd been there I would have seen her silver dress.

She must have gone back up.

I took the stairs, two at the time, hitting the top of the stairs.

After racing down the hall, I reached the door to the guest room. The room she'd used before.

I knocked and called her name.

There was no answer.

I tried the doorknob but it was locked.

What the—?

I knocked again and called out her name.

Maybe I'd missed her. Maybe she wasn't inside.

But then I heard the door unlock and it slowly opened.

Sophia stood there looking at me with watery eyes.

"Sophia," I said on a breath.

"I'm too late," she said.

"What? No. Why would you say that?"

She backed up to let me inside and shook her head.

"You've already found someone."

I stared blankly at her. I'd found someone?

"Who?" I asked.

She looked at me, then looked past me.

I turned to see Isabella standing in the doorway.

Then it all clicked together.

"No," I said. "Isabella is my sister."

"Your..." Sophia turned her back to me.

I waved my sister away and closed the door.

I walked slowly toward her and she turned, searching my eyes.

"Sophia," I said. "I would wait for you. Forever."

Then she was in my arms. I picked her up and twirled her around.

Setting her on her feet, I kissed away the tears that trailed down her cheeks.

"You're crying," I said, kissing her lips lightly.

"Happy," she said.

Then I kissed her, pressing my lips to hers. She tasted like honey. Smelled like heaven. Wild flowers and cinnamon.

I loved her taste. Her scent.

I loved her.

Putting one hand beneath her knees, I picked up her and carried her to the bed.

And this time I wasn't letting her go.

"Will you still marry me?" I asked, nuzzling her ear.

"Yes," she said breathlessly. "Yes."

"What's this?" I asked, pulling the haversack over her head.

"Some 'um supplies we might need," she said.

I grinned. My girl thought of everything.

66

SOPHIA

I woke the next morning to the sound of dogs barking and a rooster crowing. I felt relaxed. Relaxed and content.

Sunlight streamed in through the window. No evidence of last night's storm.

I put out a hand, but I was alone.

Sitting up in bed, I took in the room. No electric outlets. No light fixtures. No closet or bathroom.

I pulled my bag from the floor and pulled out a little rolled note I'd written earlier.

Taking the little pry bar I'd also brought with me, I went to the window and carefully pried up the frame. I slid the little piece of paper inside and used the pry bar to hammer it back down.

Grandpa was certain that the window frames in this room were original and had never been touched. Painted maybe. Put otherwise left as they were. Even the glass had never been changed out like it had in some of the other rooms in the house.

There. I straightened and put the pry bar back in my bag. I

didn't know if Grandpa would get that or not, but I felt better doing as we had agreed.

The door opened and Nathan stepped inside, carrying a tray.

"Good morning," he said, closing the door with his foot and setting the tray on the bed.

"Hungry?"

"Starving," I said, climbing back on the bed to sit next to him.

He placed a piece of orange in my mouth.

So good.

Instead of eating, he swept a lock of hair back from my face and watched me.

"What?" I asked.

"You're pretty."

I laughed. "You're pretty too."

"Pretty, huh?" He put his hands on my shoulders and his lips on mine.

By the time we came up for air, the sun was high in the sky. Noon.

While I got dressed, he paced to the window.

"We need to go into town," he said. "get you some clothes."

"Okay," I said, tugging on my boots. "Hopefully we'll make it this time."

"We'll make it. There's not a cloud in the sky."

I smiled.

"Do you remember meeting me? In the foyer?"

"Of course I do." He stood in front of me and ran a finger lightly over my cheek.

"How did you do it? How did you get the key to me?" I toyed with the ribbon around my neck.

"I don't know," he said. "But my mother is a Becquerel."

"Which means?"

"That means I carry Becquerel blood, just like you do."

I stared at him a moment, trying to figure out what he was saying.

"You can travel through time?"

"Theoretically," he said with a small smile. "But I think that was the extent of my time travel. I think we're supposed to live here. In this time."

"How do you know?"

He dipped down and kissed me.

"The same way I know I love you," he said against my lips.

I put my arms around him.

He was right.

I had come home.

EPILOGUE

Four months later

Nathan sat outside, his back against an oak tree. I lay on a blanket next to him, my head in his lap.

I held my Kindle, scanning through my books. I literally had hundreds of them.

He toyed with my hair.

"You know," he said. "You could design houses if you wanted to."

I grinned up at him. "I know." He didn't know I'd brought a drafting compass, a ruler, and an adjustable triangle.

He bent down and kissed the top of my head.

"Maybe later though," I said. "I think I'm going to be rather busy these next few years."

"Busy doing what?" he asked. "Reading all those books?"

"Maybe," I said. "But I'll also be teaching someone else how to read."

"Yeah? Who's that?"

I opened up a book on my Kindle.

Teach Your Child to Read.

I held it up for him to see.

He looked from the book to me and I saw the moment the realization struck.

"We're having a baby," he said, his voice full of pride.

"Yes."

He shifted me in his lap and kissed me on the lips.

If he kept kissing me like this, we were going to have a dozen babies.

He cupped my cheek with one hand.

"I love you more than life itself," he said.

"And I love you more," I said, pulling his lips back to mine.

If love was what had brought us together and what was going to keep us together, I was certain neither of us was ever going to have to worry about going to another time.

The key to the clock was hidden away in my bag, tucked in a trunk in our bedroom at our house.

He'd built that house for us and I was in the process of decorating it. It took forever for furniture to arrive. No UPS deliveries, but I had plenty of catalogues to order from.

Someday I might design and build houses again.

But right now, we were going to build a family together.

When I became an architect, I knew I wanted to build things, but I'd never known it would be a family.

Nonetheless, it was perfect for me.

Nathan was perfect for me.

He shifted and looked into my eyes.

"Sophia," he said. "Can we agree on something? About our children?"

"What?"

"Let's tell them about the time travel so it'll be normal for them."

"Good idea," I said. "We'll read them bedtime stories about it."

"You are perfect," he said before he kissed me again.

Children. We were definitely going to have lots of them.

Loved Reading about Sophia and Nathan?

Turn the page for a preview of Scripted in the Stars...

SCRIPTED IN THE STARS PREVIEW

CHAPTER 1

Prologue

Jonathan Becquerel slipped his pry bar beneath the window frame in the guest room on the second floor of his house. Sophia's room.

He moved slowly. Methodically. Careful not to break the several hundred-year-old glass panes.

One of his favorite 80s songs blared through the air pods his granddaughter Sophia had ordered for him. She'd also created a play list of his favorite songs on his phone.

Considering that Jonathan lived in the country and mostly stayed to himself, he attributed his level of being modern and hip to his granddaughter's efforts.

Though it had only been hours since he saw her, he already missed her terribly.

He'd raised the window before going to work to let some fresh air in. The soft breeze brought the scent of daffodils with it. They were his favorite flower. Not necessarily because of how they looked, though he did prefer the white ones, but because of their strong scent.

Sometimes he'd cut some out of his garden and bring them inside. Their fresh scent would perfume the house for days.

Having the window open, however, was a much better option. It allowed the scent to fill the room without having to cut the flowers. He much preferred letting them live to cutting them.

With the window frame loosened, he nudged it out with the prybar. He winced when the wood cracked. Nothing less than was expected since the window frames in this room, like the glass, were hundreds of years old.

It didn't worry him, though. He could fix it easy enough.

Since it was already cracked, he just ripped it off, letting the wood crumble.

Along with the wood, a little roll of paper—alkaline paper—dropped out. She'd thought of everything. He remembered the day the alkaline paper had been delivered. It was the same day he'd received his first packet of white daffodil bulbs.

He and Sophia had spent the afternoon outside planting them. She had been quieter that day. It had only been later that he'd learned the true reason why she'd bought the alkaline paper. They said alkaline paper could last centuries without decomposing. How they'd known that was beyond Jonathan's comprehension.

Careful with the little slip of paper, much more careful than he had been with the window frame, he unrolled it and leaned back on the stool he sat on.

Then he began to read the familiar handwriting.

Dear Jonathan,

If you are reading this letter, then you know that I have gone back in time. It worked.

I so hope you found this letter. It makes me happy that you know I've made it to the past safely.

I didn't get to say goodbye and I'm sorry for that. But we talked about this and I know you understand. Still I miss you terribly and wish that you were here with me.

Please tell the rest of the family that I love them.

Take care of yourself and know that I love you.

Sophia

Jonathan dropped his hands in his lap.

It was done then. Just as he'd known it would be.

Sophia resembled her grandmother—Jonathan's wife—in that way. And she had no man holding her here. She'd found her man in the past. Somewhere in the 1800s. His name was Nathan Laurent.

As much as he didn't want to, Jonathan knew what he had to do.

He pulled his cell phone out of his shirt pocket and scrolled through until he found his grandson's number.

It was a heavy heart that he called Cameron Becquerel.

Making this phone call drove home Jonathan's acceptance that this was real.

Sophia had really gone back in time.

Chapter 1
Cameron Becquerel

I drove my Maserati with the top down along the River Road.

I'd been on location in Memphis filming one of my screenplays when Grandpa Jonathan—my father's father—had called me.

Although he hadn't said what he needed to talk to me about, I already knew.

It had been a long time coming.

I turned down the one-lane dirt road leading to the Becquerel Estate and drove beneath the ancient oak trees with limbs so thick and heavy, they dipped all the way to the ground.

Silver gray moss clung to the trees, especially the older oaks for which they had an affinity.

A text message appeared on the dashboard in front of me.

MEGAN: *Call me sweetie. I miss you.*

Although she'd been unhappy about it, I'd left my girlfriend Megan back in Memphis.

She was upset that I wasn't bringing her to meet my Grandpa.

I'd tried to explain that he was old and in bad shape and didn't tolerate visitors.

It wasn't true of course.

Grandpa was eighty if he was a day and he was in better shape than some men half his age. His mind was good, too. He was very fortunate.

Truth was, I had some personal family business to discuss with Grandpa and I didn't want Megan to know about it.

That was the thing about working in Hollywood. I had to keep my real personal life to myself. I had, in effect, to be someone I wasn't.

Even Megan couldn't know who I really was.

The less my colleagues knew about my real personal life, the less ammunition they had to use against me.

I had a deep visceral reaction to seeing the house up ahead. It was a lovely southern Greek plantation house... hundreds of years old.

I'd thought several times about using it as a movie set. But again, as long as my Grandpa lived, which I hoped was forever, I would keep it away from my life as a screenwriter.

And Megan, one of the stars of the current film I was working on was part of the me I wanted to project to the world. A tall leggy blonde with a sultry, knowing smile. The star of my current project. Not that I was complaining. She was good in bed.

I pulled around behind the house and parked next to the back veranda. Grandpa had his garden back in shape again. Granted it was ten times smaller than it had been the last time I was here, but he'd obviously been working on it. That was a good sign.

I parked the car and hit the button to put the top up.

I halfway expected Grandpa to be sitting out on the veranda, but there was nothing but three empty white wooden rockers.

I knocked on the door and turned around, looking toward the river.

Only a glimpse of the river was barely visible from here, through the trees. The water glimmered beneath the setting sun, the first sign of the sunset to come.

I turned around as the door opened.

Grandpa stood there, a blank expression on his face and pushed the door open.

I stepped through and closed the door behind me.

We walked silently into the kitchen and stood looking at each other.

"Did they find her body?" I asked.

Chapter 2
Isabella Laurent

Near Natchez, Mississippi
May 1853

It was a beautiful clear night. The sun had dipped below the horizon leaving the moon to watch over us.

The Becquerel home was lit up like day light with candles and lanterns everywhere.

Fresh flowers filled the house with color and a sweet scent that tempered the scent of cigar smoke and the ham that had been smoking for most of the day, making my mouth water.

The grandfather clock began to chime the hour. I would have to go down soon. Actually I was already teetering on arriving too late.

Two of my brothers were already downstairs, no doubt finding some kind of trouble to get into.

My other brother, Nathan, was probably at his own home with his wife Sophia. Sometimes they came to the parties, sometimes they didn't. My brother Nathan was like me when it came to parties. He could live just fine without them.

I stood at the top of the stairs, out of the way, watching the guests as they arrived.

This was the third party my cousins had held in the last month, always eager to introduce me to eligible men.

Mon Dieu.

Didn't they understand that I was not in the market for a husband?

I had given some serious thought to hiding out in my cousin's garçonnière for the evening or maybe pleading off with a bad headache, but getting a new dress was worth enduring an evening of music.

Besides, Momma knew me well enough to keep me in check. I could get nothing past her.

This one had the widest hoop skirt I'd ever worn. And it had a million yards of silk cascading over it. But the best part was the perfect décolletage that revealed a scandalously large swatch of my creamy white skin. Wearing this dress, I felt all grown up and maybe, just maybe, I'd try out some of those feminine wiles my governess had been insisting that I learn.

Like she said, I didn't have to marry them or even let them court me just because I flirted a bit with them.

I sighed. If nothing else, it would help pass the time.

These soirees could be so tiresomely long. If I hadn't been certain that Momma would swat me on the head, I would have brought a book downstairs with me.

Momma allowed me a lot of leniencies, but that wasn't one she would tolerate. A lady always showed good manners, no matter what situation she found herself in.

"Miss?" Villars, the butler asked, coming up behind me. "Is there anything I can get for you?"

"No thank you Villars," I said.

Villars put his hands behind his back and stood still for a moment.

"It's a lovely night for a storm," he said.

Perplexed by his words, I turned to look at him, but he was walking away.

Whatever did he mean by that?

I shrugged and started downstairs.

I'd always found my cousins in the northern part of Mississippi to be somewhat strange and in the few months I'd lived here with my family, that had not changed.

However, being from New Orleans, I had a high tolerance for strangeness.

Chapter 3
Cameron

Grandpa heated water the old-fashioned way with a tea kettle on the stovetop.

Hot tea wasn't something I typically bothered with. I usually ended my day with a glass of red wine. But if there was one thing I'd learned working in Hollywood, it was to be flexible and low maintenance.

There was very little I despised more than a prima donna, especially in a man.

Being raised by a general had taught me at a very young age that a man's job was to be part of the team and to defer to authority or in this case authority would be synonymous with my elders.

The tea kettle whistled and Grandpa went over to turn off the flame. He moved a bit slower than I would have like to see.

Maybe he'd called me here about something other than my sister. Maybe he wanted to discuss his own health.

Grandpa was at that age when he needed to consider his options. I hated the thought of him having to leave here to go into assisted living. If he needed someone to come here to help him out, I could hire a live-in caregiver. We could either move his bedroom downstairs or put in an elevator.

I glanced around. My sister had been the architect. She was the one who would have known how to incorporate an elevator into a house like this.

Fortunately there were other architects and I could easily make it happen. If that was what he wanted.

"Do you get lonely out here?" I asked.

"What?" He turned around with two mugs of steaming hot tea. "Hardly. I have—"

He stopped in mid-sentence and slid into the chair across from me.

I had a sense, a tingling along my spine, that there was something else. Something he had to tell me.

Maybe it was because I wrote fictional scripts for a living. I had a tendency to look ahead for possibilities.

"There's something I need to tell you," he said. "Something that is probably long overdue." He slid one of the mugs over toward me.

I held the mug close and breathed in the minty scented steam with a new appreciation for hot tea.

"Does this have something to do with Sophia?"

My sister Sophia had gone missing ten years ago. It had shattered my family to the core.

But with time we'd gone forward. Moved on with our lives.

In some ways it had made us closer, but in other ways it had put a wall between us.

Even though it had happened here, under Grandpa's watch so to speak, he'd been overall quiet. He'd called me.

Our mother lived in France with her new husband and my father, still wrapped up in military retirement, was starting a new life as well, with his new wife.

As the oldest of four siblings, responsibility tended to fall on my shoulders anyway, so I was used to it.

But dealing with the disappearance of my sister was another thing entirely.

I'd never been the same.

"Yes," he said, obviously stalling.

"Grandpa," I said. "Just tell me. Whatever it is, I can handle it. I've come to terms with the reality that she will not be coming back.

Grandpa sipped his tea and looked into my eyes. He didn't believe me. Whatever it was, it was so bad he didn't believe I could handle it.

I braced myself. Prepared for the worst. The worst I could think of was they'd found her body in the woods or the river. Though how that had happened after ten years was more than I could imagine.

"She went back in time," he said.

Keep reading Scripted in the Stars…

Kathryn Kaleigh is the author of sixty-eight novels, over one hundred short stories, and many collections.

kathrynkaleigh.com

www.ingramcontent.com/pod-product-compliance
Lightning Source LLC
Chambersburg PA
CBHW020325030826
48979CB00020B/86

* 9 7 8 1 6 4 7 9 1 3 9 2 2 *